things you
either hate or love

Also by Brigid Lowry

Follow the Blue

Guitar Highway Rose

things
you either
hate or love

BRIGID LOWRY

Holiday House / New York

First published in Australia in 2005 by Allen & Unwin Pty Ltd.,
83 Alexander Street, Crows Nest NSW 2065, Australia
under the title *With Lots of Love from Georgia*.
First published in the United States of America
by Holiday House, Inc. in 2006
All Rights Reserved
Printed in the United States of America
www.holidayhouse.com
First Edition
1 3 5 7 9 10 8 6 4 2
Text design by Sandra Nobes
Set in 11 pt Bembo by Tou-Can Design

Library of Congress Cataloging-in-Publication Data
Lowry, Brigid.
Things you either hate or love / Brigid Lowry.—1st ed.
p. cm.
Summary: A cynical, overweight, and lonely Australian teenager spends
her summer vacation making lists, eating comfort foods, and trying
to earn enough money to attend a big rock concert.
ISBN-13: 978-0-8234-2004-9
ISBN-10: 0-8234-2004-3
[1. Overweight persons—Fiction.
2. Summer employment—Fiction. 3. Australia—Fiction.]
I. Title.
PZ7.L96725Th 2006
[Fic]—dc22
2005052539

Acknowledgments

Gratitude to the Dunedin College of Education for my
writing residency, on which I reworked this book, and
to the Robert Lord Trust, for my time at Titan Street.

Big ups to Nick Pratt for letting me plunder his toilet paper
poem, and to Yvette Walker for her brilliant contribution
to the list of *Things You Can't See*.

To Lynne Dowdeswell and Laurel Shaw-Adams. I appreciate you
sharing your lives with me more than you will ever know.

Thank you John Marsden for letting me steal some list ideas
from your terrific book *Everything I Know About Writing*.

Kisses for my women friends, who love me even though
I'm neurotic and worry about my hair all the time.

Eternal gratitude to Paul and Sam for believing in me.

Bravo to my editors, Rosalind Price and Sue Flockhart,
for their patience and wisdom.

things you
either hate or love

starlight boulevarde of dreams

My name is Georgia. ❀ I live in a town called Anywhere that has too many shopping malls and not enough skate parks. I'm taller than most fifteen year old girls and I weigh more too. I have wavy red hair that does what it pleases, and my eyes change colour in different lights, from hazelnut to tawny green. I like to think of myself as a brilliant creative person, but sometimes I just feel like a sad lonely girl with a big bum.

It's a drifty summer afternoon and I'm lying on my bed thinking about Jakob, who, as everyone knows, is the lead singer of Natural Affinity. I have adored him forever – well, for over a year, anyway. I've stuck a huge poster of him beside my bed, draped it with a silvery blue sari and surrounded it with glow-in-the-dark stars. It's my Jakob shrine.

When Mum asks me why I like him so much I can't explain it properly. I just do. He looks like the kind of person who loves dogs, reads books and is a vegetarian. He's a melancholy poet with skinny fingers, and when he plays guitar my whole world shines. He's my amazing rhythm ace, my blue moon dancer, the prince of my heart.

1

Hayley and Fifi are the other two members of Natural Affinity. They're sisters. I read in *Rolling Stone* that Jakob and Fifi are an item, which is a total bummer, although I can see why he would fancy her. She's slender with blonde dreadlocks. Beautiful, in a sulky sort of way. Fifi plays electric piano, Hayley plays tambourine and percussion, and they both sing back-up vocals. Hayley has heaps of piercings and very short green hair. It looks like lawn. She's supposed to be a lesbian. I wouldn't want to kiss her though. You could do a lot of damage with that pierced tongue of hers. I don't know how Fifi manages to sleep properly with those lumpy dreads. Having to be fashionable sucks. I can't be bothered wearing uncomfortable stuff such as tight bras and high heels.

I wish I lived in another time and place, when big round bodies were the fashion. Maybe in Paris in 1892. I can see myself, on my balcony, picking a red geranium from my window box, waving to the handsome boy across the street. How plump and lovely she is, he thinks, as he waves back. I breakfast on buttery croissants, hot chocolate and peaches, wearing a cream silk kimono and slippers embroidered with golden birds. Or maybe Tahiti, in Gauguin's time, when women were big and brown and strong and no one wanted them to be any different.

Ah, get a grip, Georgia. You live in the wrong century. You'll never look good in an outfit that displays your podgy tummy. You were born with hair that looks like a mad cloud and eyes that are too small for your face. In this world of skinny you just don't fit. Dreams are free, but I need money. Five hundred bucks, to be precise. I have to get to a concert.

the worst time of year

I, Georgia Reeves of Golden Bay, of sound mind with a few batty bits, hereby declare that Christmas sucks. Here's the thing. Adults get seriously weird. Stress and crabbiness prevail, but you're meant to be joyous and sing cheery carols about Good King Wenceslas, whoever he was, and send people cheery cards that say Peace on Earth. You have to buy everyone a present, even though you don't have any money. In return, you get a random assortment of items, as follows.

One pretty nightie from Mum. Also some lemon fizzy whizzy bath products. Why doesn't she get it? I'm not that sort of person, and no amount of buying me girly stuff will change me into one.

An assortment of chocolates and lollies, beautifully wrapped in green and gold tissue and tied with classy gold ribbon, from Aunty Joy and Uncle Kevin. It's typical of my aunt to wrap something budget in an elegant way. Although I am a lumpy girl it doesn't mean I like low-grade confectionery.

A book voucher from Grandpa Joseph. He gives me the same thing every year because he knows I love buying art books. Good one.

My other grandparents, the revolting Reeves, sent the usual expensive card. *Happy Christmas, Georgia. Love, Grandmother and Pop.* They never send a gift. Instead they put money into a fund for me but I can't get hold of it until I'm twenty-one and it has to be used for educational purposes.

Ten bucks from my cousin, Gilda, tucked in a card featuring red roses and zappy blue hearts. It's a cool card but ten dollars won't go very far towards my goal, which is to get myself to the Natural Affinity concert in May. I only have forty dollars in the bank and I owe Mum ten bucks. As you can see, I am verging on bankruptcy.

My best gifts were Grandad's book voucher, a CD from Mel, and a drawing of an angel playing a violin from Penny, Mum's best friend.

The worst present was a journal from my aunt, Sooze. Her name is Susan but she's fond of reinventing herself. Sooze didn't spend Christmas with us this year, she went to a hippie festival at Byron Bay to learn Tibetan goat horn carving and other useful stuff. I bet someone gave her the journal and because the yellow satin cover didn't resonate with her aura she fobbed it off on me. I've decided to give it to someone else. If they don't want it they can pass it along as well. It can go around and around forever, the Famous Unwanted Christmas Gift.

At least she didn't give me another small container. Every year, from when I was seven to fourteen, Sooze sent me a series of little boxes: one from China, one from India, several from the Two Dollar Shop. Mum semi-tactfully asked her not to, in the end, because I'm not really into knick knacks and they just sat around gathering dust. A CD is a good present, a fifty dollar note is a good present. They should teach this stuff at Aunty School.

I'm not in favour of writing in journals. Having to write stuff at school has put me off self-expression. The teachers give you dumb topics and then scrawl all over your work with red pen, covering it with trivial corrections and derogatory comments, so what's the use?

'Georgia tends to lack focus and is sometimes a little too creative,' Mrs Jellicoe, my English teacher, wrote on my report last year. Stuff her. Anyone who sets 'My life as a

things you either

Household Appliance/Your Choice,' as an essay topic deserves to die. I thought I did pretty well, although maybe I went a little too far choosing a vibrator. I wish we could write reports on the teachers.

'Mrs Jellicoe has extremely dodgy dress sense and a tendency to spit.'

'Mr Noble has no sense of humour. He could lose a little weight.'

Hey, don't get me started. Actually, I kind of like Mrs Jellicoe. She tells us interesting stuff, like how writing in the present tense gives narrative a more direct impact. She also says carrying the right handbag is the most important fashion statement a woman can make, and that dairy products are poison to your digestive system. Some of her ideas are from lah-lah land, but she knows a bit about English. Her lessons are fun, because she forgets what she's supposed to be teaching and tells us stories from her happy years spent backpacking around Italy, Turkey and Greece. Her nostalgia for the person she used to be makes the time pass quicker. As far as I'm concerned, she's the one who lacks focus, but if it means we can meander around Europe for an entire period, who's complaining?

I've had another idea about what to do with that journal. One day when I get really bored I'll fill its creamy pages with fairytales about dead princesses and smart-arse princes, wicked stepfathers and hairy little goblins with bad tempers.

⚘

Anyway, this is what happened on Christmas day at our house.

'We three kings of Orient are, one had a suitcase, one a guitar, dah dah dah, dah dah dah dee dah, following yonder star.' Uncle Kevin sings loudly and slightly out of tune as he stands at the barbecue, aimlessly turning the sausages. Singing is his attempt at Christmas cheer, but it doesn't fool me. He's skolling his beer fast, and he keeps glancing at his watch, even though he and Aunty Joy and Gilda have just arrived. He'd much rather be pottering around in his shed but it's a family Christmas, folks, so we all have to pretend to enjoy ourselves and get through it as best we can. Aunty Joy scurries back and forth like a mad rabbit, fiddling with the table decorations and rearranging the salads. Special occasions make her even more nervous than usual.

'Shouldn't the flame be a bit lower, dear? They look as if they're burning.'

'They're fine, sweetie.' Uncle Kevin wipes his face on his shirt and swigs the last of his can. The day just keeps getting hotter, so he's sweating a lot, but it's probably the beer as well as the heat.

'Not on your shirt, Kevin love,' my aunt nags, then scoots away before he can reply. He pretends not to hear, and prods the sausages so he can fit the fish and prawns on the grill.

'Blast,' he mutters, as a sausage rolls onto the ground.

Aunty Joy and Uncle Kevin don't get on. The saddest bit is that they call each other all this sweetie darling stuff, as if it will disguise their wobbly relationship. Being around them is a pain, which is why Gilda is hiding out in the lounge reading a *Who* magazine she brought with her. Gilda is eighteen, three years older than me. She is thin and pale, with wispy blonde hair and a liking for pastel colours. Sometimes I think she will fade away altogether.

Theoretically I am supposed to be helping, but it's all done, except for the stuff on the grill, so I'm just hanging around waiting for the food. My mother is a very organised

things you either

person. She stayed up late last night, roasting capsicums and making potato salad and raspberry cheesecake. Now she's in the kitchen, drinking champagne and poking around in the fridge to see if she's forgotten anything. At first the bubbly will cheer her up in a tinselly sort of way but later she will end up crying, like she always does, because it's at Christmas she misses my father the most.

Uncle Kevin has covered the barbequed food with a piece of foil. Now he's topping up the glasses of bubbly so it'll be ages until we're actually allowed to eat anything. We're waiting for Grandad, who's always late, so I go inside and talk to Gilda.

'God, I'm starving. Are you?'

'Not really,' she says. 'Dad made pancakes for breakfast. I'll be into those prawns though.'

'I like your top.' She's wearing a peach singlet, trimmed with lace. It suits her.

'Thanks. Santa gave it to me, but I chose it.'

'What are you reading about?'

'Butt inserts.'

'Whaat?'

'Bottom enhancements. Increases your butt cheeks, makes them round, like Beyonce Knowles.'

'I'm way ahead then. I'm already there,' I say, slapping my hand on my bum. Gilda smiles, but she looks sad. 'I'm not into plastic surgery, are you?' I continue.

'Nah, not really. Except for medical reasons.'

'Cleft palates and stuff. Yeah, for sure. Who needs three ears and a huge birthmark, anyhow?'

Gilda gives me a wan smile. Something's troubling her.

'What's up, Gilds?'

'Nothing.'

'Come on, give it up. You seem miserable. What's the matter?'

'The usual. Mum and Dad. You know what they're like. Christmas sends Mum into stress overdrive. Dad tries to please her but ends up resentful. Mostly I can ignore it but sometimes it just gets to me.'

'Poor you.' I go over and give her a clumsy hug. She's frail and bony, but she gives me a friendly squeeze in return. I'm glad I made the effort.

'Don't worry about it. Nothing you can do. Thanks for asking.' She sticks her head back into the world of glitzy trash. I hesitate, then leave her to it. There's something I have to do. It's time.

⚘

I go upstairs and scrabble around in my wardrobe. Pull out the battered cardboard box, dotted with silver stars and lined with black velvet, made when I was seven, in which I hide my treasures. A curl of my baby hair. A dried seahorse. A smooth oval of rose quartz. The silver filigree brooch, shaped like a palm tree, which belonged to my nana. A ruby earring I found in a park. Three photographs of my father. My mother has albums, and there's a big portrait of the two of them in the hall, taken the day they got married. But these three are mine.

A toddler in a knitted cardigan, laughing as he runs across a lawn.

Fourteen years old, on a horse.

A passport photo, aged twenty. He looks sad in this one, as if he knows he won't get to travel to all the places he dreams of.

I prop the photos against the box and carefully arrange

things you either

my treasures in front. Then I light a white candle and sit quietly for a while. This is my Christmas ritual. Nobody but me knows about it. A small silent space. For my dad.

♥

My father, Michael, came from a family who made big money breeding racehorses. He was handsome. Tall and dark, like a well-bred stallion. Anna, my mother, was from a different sort of family: a muddly one, with too much noise and not enough money. There were three kids, my mum, Joy and Sooze. My grandad owned a second-hand shop that didn't have many customers. The yard was cluttered with rusty truck parts, and broken furniture that he never got around to mending. My nana was a large woman with a mournful heart who spent her whole life missing Ireland and finding things 'a trouble'. When everything got too much for her she took to her bed for days on end, like a beached whale.

My mother left home on her eighteenth birthday. She went nursing, and on her very first day on the wards she met my father. He'd been kicked by a horse and was in overnight for observation. My mother always stops here when she tells me this story, and sighs a dreamy sigh.

'Was it love at first sight?' I ask her, every time.

'It was love at first sight,' she replies. 'Yes, it certainly was.'

Three weeks later they were married, even though his snobby parents didn't approve of my mother, and refused to come to the wedding. My mother and father loved each other, and they were happy. My dad got a job selling advertising. He was good at it; he could charm the pants off anyone.

'Yeah, Mum, he sure charmed them off you.'

'Georgie!' she says, but she smiles.

'When you came along we were the proudest parents in the whole wide world. We lived at Garnet Road, in a weatherboard cottage with a red door, a verandah and a hedge of blue hydrangeas.'

I know about that. I can't remember much about my father, but I remember sunlight and warmth and laughing. I remember the beach, and having a sandy bum. I remember a red door, and blue petals, and a big pair of feet. I think I do, anyhow.

One day when I was four years old, my father came home from work and said he didn't feel very well so he was going upstairs to lie down. When my mother went to tell him dinner was ready, he was dead. He'd had a massive brain haemorrhage. There wasn't any reason for it or anything. Sometimes it just happens — that's what the doctors told my mum.

He's buried at Golden Hill Cemetery, next to an oak tree.

Michael David Reeves. 1957 – 1988. *Gone to God*, it says on the speckled marble headstone. I think it should just say Gone.

Since then there's just been the two of us. Mainly my mother just gets on with life, but special times like Christmas and birthdays are hard for her. She pretends to be festive but her pain leaks out. So that's why Christmas sucks. Tis the season to be jolly, tra la la la la, la la la la.

❀

Finally Uncle Kevin yells out 'Grub's up.' I hurry downstairs and am scooped up for a big hug by Grandpa, who's finally arrived. I love his peppery smell. He's spruced himself up

things you either

for the occasion by ironing his baggy old trousers. Mum comes out of the kitchen, with her glass in one hand and the lemon mayonnaise in the other. Aunty Joy drags Gilda away from her magazine and we all sit down to eat. My aunt insists on saying a very long, boring grace. She blathers on about the meaning of family, emphasising how nice it would be if Sooze were here. Yeah right. Those two may be sisters but hostility hovers when they're together. I roll my eyes at Grandpa, who's adjusting his hearing aid. He gives me a wink. At last we're allowed to eat.

The BEST THING about lunch:
the yummy food

The WORST THINGS about lunch:
having to wear silly paper hats
doing heaps of washing up
the following conversation:

'So, Georgie, how's life?'
'Good.'
'How's school going?'
'Yeah, okay.' It's the holidays, dimwit, I think, but I try to sound friendly. Uncle Kev means well.
'Georgie will be in Year 11 next year,' my mother adds. My uncle is making polite conversation to fill the gap between the prawns and the pudding. I don't imagine it makes much difference to him whether I'm in Year 11 or Year 97.
'How's your savings plan coming along, then?'
I wish I'd never told Gilda about my plan to fly to Melbourne to see Natural Affinity at the big May Day concert. I also wish she hadn't told her parents. Uncle

Kevin asks me about my savings plan every time he sees me and the news is never good.

'Not brilliant, actually.'

'Naked Affinity, hey? They must be really hot.'

'It's Natural Affinity, Dad,' Gilda says wearily. It can't be easy having the least cool father in the whole world. His Christmas outfit is a Hawaiian shirt and a clean pair of shorts. Need I say more?

'Five hundred dollars is a lot of money,' he continues, stating the obvious.

'Yeah,' I say. 'But it's not just the concert ticket, it's my airfare, and a night in a hostel.'

'So, how much *have* you saved, dear?' Aunty Joy asks, wiping her nose surreptitiously on her sparkly gold serviette.

'Not much actually. I've got forty bucks in the bank but I owe Mum ten dollars.'

Technically I should give Mum the cash Gilda gave me but it won't be easy handing that over. Christmas money is sacred.

Gilda takes another mince tart and picks the pastry lid off, then crumbles it into tiny fragments and moves them aimlessly around her plate. I can see my mother thinking, What a waste of a mince tart, as clearly as if it were written on her forehead in purple crayon. I drift off into a fantasy where everyone's thoughts are written on their foreheads in purple crayon, but I'm called back to reality with a nasty jolt.

'I have a really great idea!' Aunty Joy smiles brightly. She has a crumb stuck to her top lip. 'Why don't you get yourself a part-time job, Georgia? Babysitting perhaps, or at a bakery or a supermarket?'

Silly cow, I think. Glad that isn't written on my forehead. Mum gave me a lecture before they arrived about being

things you either

polite and I'm trying to oblige, but Aunty Joy is the most irritating person on the planet. Her sugary niceness feels false, and she doesn't listen. She asks you something and glazes over when you answer, then later asks you the same thing again. The fact that her name's Joy is one of life's more obvious little ironies. Mum finds her difficult, but she won't talk about it. 'The relationship between sisters is complex,' is all she ever says.

Actually, Aunty Joy has a point, but it's the way she makes it that bugs me. Something in her tone manages to insinuate that I'm a lazy slob who should have got myself a job some time ago.

'Good plan,' I say. 'What a really great idea.' I give her my cheesiest grin, but I drag out the 'ea' of *great* as long as I can.

'Georgia!' says my mother sharply. 'Put the kettle on, and make some coffee. And bring out the truffles while you're at it. They're in the fridge.'

'Truffles, eh?' asks Uncle Kevin. 'Don't know if I can eat another thing. You've done us proud today, Anna. I'm pretty much as stuffed as a man could be.'

Yeah, really, I think. You were stuffed the day you married Aunty Joy. Trying not to snigger, I nip off to the kitchen and eat five rum truffles while I make the coffee.

❧

do you want fries with that?

When I go down to breakfast my mother is sad. You can taste it, even though it's invisible.

'Good morning, girl child,' she says.

'Hey Mum.'

'There's no cereal, you'll have to have toast.'

I make myself four slices of raisin toast, butter them thickly and dribble a splodge of honey in my coffee. My tummy feels empty. Partly it is hunger, partly it is dread. I don't know how to deal with her sorrow sometimes.

'So, jobs,' I say, chomping into my toast. 'I hate to admit it but Aunty Joy is right. No use waiting for money to fall from the sky. What I need is a part-time job.'

'How about McDonald's? They're always advertising and it isn't far. You could go on your bike.'

'God, Mum! I can't believe you even suggested it. Mel's sister, Sandy, worked there for two weeks. She said it totally sucks. Nah, greasy burger land is not for me. I'd rather be dead.'

'There's no need to be so melodramatic, Georgia.' My mother sighs in that annoying way of hers, then tries again. 'Babysitting?'

'Maybe.' The idea doesn't exactly thrill me but I guess it would be a start.

'Or what about pamphlets?'

'Yeah, right. You get paid seventeen dollars for delivering, like, ten million. No way.'

'It would be easy money though. All you have to do is walk, and it would be good exercise.'

'I said *no way*, Mum. Didn't you hear me? Trudging up and down all those hills in the boiling hot sun and the pouring rain with a heavy bag...nah, forget it.' I'm getting ratty, so she backs off, then has a final try.

'What about a video shop? Or New World?'

'Yeah, maybe.' I pick up my plate and cup. I'll finish my brekkie in my bedroom, in peace. 'Might try a bakery,' I say as I head out the door. 'All those pastries would be nice.'

things you either

One of the not-so-wonderful things about my mother is that she's always trying to be helpful. Sometimes I really appreciate the things she does for me, but at times it feels very controlling. I've just settled myself on the bed, which has involved some radical moves, like sweeping a big heap of clothes onto the floor, and turning on my CD player with one finger while not dropping my toast or spilling my coffee. As I get comfy on my pillows I hear her little *tap tap tap* on the door. At least I've trained her to not just barge in any more. A girl needs her privacy.

'Georgie?'

'Yeah, what?'

'Can I come in?'

'Mmm.'

'I'll just turn this down a bit, okay? I've had a brainwave.'

'Mmm.' She's always turning my music down, which shits me, and I'm suspicious about my mother's brainwaves. But she's looking helpful and sad at the same time, like a spaniel, so I give her a smile and listen up.

'What about the Masons?' she asks.

'Eh?' For one weird moment I think my mother is suggesting I join a secret society for businessmen who like wearing elk heads.

'Natalie Mason, the new woman at work. She's got three kids. I could ask her about babysitting if you like.'

Kids = babysitting = money. Oh what the hell. Why not?

'Yeah, all right. Check it out if you want. Thanks, Mum. Turn the music up as you leave, okay?'

I ring my friend Mel and make a plan to go to her house, and I forget all about babysitting until Saturday morning, when I come down sleepily for almond croissants and fresh orange juice. It's our weekend ritual, which also requires a pot of coffee, plenty of time and a big fat newspaper. I get the Travel Section first, Mum gets Lifestyle, and then we swap. Beautiful.

'You haven't forgotten about tonight, have you?'

'Nah,' I lie.

'You have to be there at 7 o'clock. I'll drive you over and Nat's husband, Alan his name is, will bring you home. They won't be late. They're going to a play and they'll definitely be home by midnight.'

'How much do I charge them again?' I ask, not wanting to admit that I only have a vague memory of the conversation we've had about this. Mum tried to talk to me while I was watching *Charmed*, which is a bad habit I haven't trained her out of yet.

'Six dollars an hour. It should be easy money. The kids go to bed by eight, and you can watch TV the rest of the night, or read or something.

'Sweet,' I say. Easy money is the kind of money I like.

my first thirty dollars

Mum drops me off on her way to Wild Women, which is a choir. It's her first night, and she's kind of jittery. It must be catching. As she drives off I contemplate running away, down the leafy street, to start a new life as a juggler and trapeze artist in a travelling circus. I follow this idea into a world of glittery costumes and radiant applause, until I go too far and see myself flying through the air, missing my partner's hands and thumping to the ground in front of the jeering crowd. So instead I walk slowly up the path, trying not to talk to the petunias, and knock on the door.

things you either

Natalie opens it. She's a bouncy blonde who seems to enjoy hair products, and she's wearing a black lace dress and fishnet stockings. She resembles a high class hooker rather than a suburban mother, but as my purple track pants don't fit properly and my huge grey t-shirt makes me look like a baggy saggy elephant, who am I to judge?

'Hello, you must be Georgia, come on in. The kids are dying to meet you, aren't you, kids?'

Actually, no. A skinny boy of about eight, wearing Wiggles pyjamas, and an older girl in a pinky-orange nightie are sitting on the steps regarding me doubtfully, while a toddler with a runny nose is refusing to come out from behind his mother's legs.

'This is Stephanie, that's Liam, and this is Joe. Let go, Joey. Look, here's Georgia. You're going to be a good boy for her, aren't you, darling? Let go, I said.'

The chilling tone of her final 'Let go' worked wonders, which was good, because he was just about to wipe a slimy goober all over the hem of her dress.

'We should get going, Nat. Parking is going to be an issue.'

The father person has arrived. He's handsome, in a Ken-doll sort of a way, and anyone who says 'issue' in that context is a wanker as far as I'm concerned. But there's no time to worry about the finer points of the English language because Natalie is telling me about bed times and snack foods and I'm trying to look intelligent and trustworthy. She jots down her mobile number and they're gone. It's just me and three children standing in a lounge room.

'We don't need a babysitter,' Stephanie says sulkily. 'I'm eleven.'

'You're fat,' volunteers Liam, glaring at me. Joey just stares.

I'm thinking hard and fast, mainly that I should have taken the running-away-to-the-circus option more seriously. Then, suddenly, an idea.

'Here's the thing,' I begin. 'If you don't behave, I'm going home. Right now. You'll be all by yourselves and the boogie monsters will creep around and peer in the windows at you. They might even come inside. When your parents get home they'll be so angry with you for being mean to the babysitter that they'll cut off your ears and lock you away without food for a thousand years. *Or* you can behave. It's entirely up to you.'

I pause. This could go either way. If anyone says 'Cool. Go home,' I'll be completely screwed. Suddenly Stephanie bursts into giggles.

'Wanna see my room?'

'Sure,' I grin. 'Come on, guys.'

Stephanie's bedroom is a dazzling tribute to the colour pink. A sparkly heart mobile dangles over the bed, which has a rose-pink satin quilt and is neatly arranged with heart-shaped pillows, fluffy rabbits, several pink-clad Barbies and a giant Minnie Mouse. There's a pink and gold parasol, a mauve dressing gown dotted with pale pink daisies, a tulip-patterned box of pink tissues and a big cardboard clock with a crimson rose on the face. Even the filmy curtains are made out of luminous ruby netting. I'm not a big fan of pink. I should hate this room, but I don't. If you want to be a girly princess you might as well go for it.

'Pretty cool room,' I say. 'Is your room blue, Joey?'

'Nah, his room is a pigsty.'

'You mean yours is, broccoli brains!'

'Come on, no fighting. Hey, this looks fun. Let's play Pick Up Sticks.'

18   *things you either*

Our game is not a success. Joey is too little. His chubby fingers can only manage to pick up the solo sticks near the edge, so he soon becomes fidgety. Liam tries to cheat by pretending not to see the sticks move during his go, and Stephanie is so skilled that her turns go on forever.

'What other games do you like?' I ask them.

'Monopoly,' Stephanie volunteers, but Liam doesn't agree.

'Yuck. Boring.' His face resembles an angry little pug dog. 'Woof woof,' I would like to bark but I'm being paid to be sensible tonight.

'How about you, Joey? What do you like playing?'

'I like Milo,' he answers shyly, sticking his finger up his nose in an exploratory fashion.

'I've never heard of that one. Is it like Uno?'

Joey stares at me, puzzled, and wipes some silvery slime on his pyjama sleeve.

'He means he wants some Milo to drink, duh brain!'

'Thanks for that, Liam,' I say sweetly. 'Come on, Joey, I'll get you a tissue and then you can help me make us all a drink. You big kids can watch TV.'

'Kids are baby goats, my dad says.' I ignore him. I'm liking Liam less and less but Stephanie is beginning to seem like my kind of girl.

'Come on, idiot boy,' she yells, grabbing Liam and hauling him down the stairs by his pyjama collar.

We sprawl around in the lounge watching TV, drinking thick creamy Milo and chomping on the banana muffins that Natalie has left for us. They're kind of dry, so we put loads of butter on them, and lots of raspberry jam.

'More Milo?' Joey asks, holding out his empty cup. I'm not sure that more is a good idea, but he adds 'Please?' so sweetly that I relent and make him some more. I like this little guy, apart from the snot factor.

'More on top,' he instructs, climbing up on the bench to watch me. 'I like it with crunchy bits on top.'

'Like this?' I sprinkle a big scoop on top of his drink.

'Yes indeedy, Mr Tweedy.' He has a loud chuckle at his own joke, and back we go to the lounge. Joey snuggles up beside me on the couch. This is what a little brother would be like, I think. It's nice. We surf channels until we find a reality show about a family who live on a desert island for a year. So far they've been there for three weeks and they hate it. It's very silly but it keeps us amused until 8.30. Natalie said to put Joey to bed at eight, and the others at nine, but I split the difference.

'Okay, bed time. Clean your teeth, everyone, and go to the toilet. I'll read you a story, Joey, and you guys can read in bed for a while.'

'That sucks,' grumbles Liam. 'It's only half past eight…'

'Just do it,' I say crisply. He opens his mouth to complain when all of a sudden the lights go out. The telly goes off too, and there we are, in the silent dark.

'Oops,' I say, trying to sound calm, which I totally do not feel. 'It must be a power cut, but don't worry. It'll be all right. Sit tight while I see if the whole street is out, or just us.' I stumble over to the window, knock my knee on the corner of the coffee table, peer out into the gloom.

'Well, it's not just this house. The whole street's dark. That's good. It means someone will be ringing to report it. The power will probably come on again soon – it usually does. Stephanie, do you know where your mum keeps candles?'

'Um, not really. I've got a big candle in my room though.'

things you either

'Okay, stay here. I'll go and get it. Where are matches kept, does anyone know?'

'I'll get some.' Before I have time to say no, Liam scurries off, nimbly making his way through the darkness. I follow, clumsily, feeling my way round an obstacle course of shadowy shapes. I lumber up the stairs, glad they're thickly carpeted. Stephanie's room is a murky cave but luckily I remember where the candle is. I noticed it earlier on her dressing table, next to a glass Swan Lake music box and a picture of Britney Spears. I grope around, trying not to knock anything over, glad when my fingers meet the cool smooth wax. Then I stumble back to the lounge. Liam's already there, delightedly flicking away on a cigarette lighter. I don't dare ask where he got it. Probably under his bed next to his cigarettes.

Together we light the candle. It doesn't give much light but at least now I can see their faces. Liam looks thrilled. Stephanie looks worried, and Joey is the wrong colour, pale as paper.

'I feel sick.' Straightaway he chucks up, all over his pyjamas and slippers. It's gruesome. Even by candlelight, you can see bits of jammy muffin in it.

Mum is still up when Mr Ken Doll drops me home just after midnight. She's sitting at the kitchen table, reading a magazine and drinking peppermint tea.

'How did it go?' she greets me, all cheery and hopeful. Natalie will spill the beans anyway so I might as well tell her what happened.

'Not great, actually. Can I have some of that tea, Mum? I feel a bit queasy.'

'Sure. What's up, love?'

'It was a nightmare. The lights went out and the little kid spewed all over the place.'

'Did you manage to clean it up okay?'

'Yeah, but it wasn't a lot of fun. The power came on again quite soon, which helped. I put all the sicky stuff in the washing machine and gave Joey a bath. The kids took ages going to sleep, though, and the lounge room smells pretty putrid.'

'Yikes, what a terrible introduction to babysitting.'

'Put it this way, Mama, there won't be a second time. Here, do these smell of sick?'

I hold out my pay, a crumpled twenty dollar note and a crisp ten. Everything, including the money and my hands, seems to have a faint foul fragrance, unless I'm imagining it. Either way, that lemon shower gel is coming out of its shiny wrapper tonight.

'How was choir?' I yell as I head towards the bathroom.

'It was great fun. There were lots of neat women there, funky ones with interesting hair.'

'Ripper,' I yell. 'Night, Mum.'

I stay in the shower until the water starts to run cold and I smell like a lemon. I slip into my big comfy nightdress and get into bed.

'Good night, Jakob. I just had the worst night. Don't even ask! I will say this, though. I'm a hundred percent glad I don't have brothers and sisters,' I tell him sleepily as I snuggle down between my satin sheets.

hanging out with mel

Mel thinks it's hilarious when I tell her all about my first and last attempt at babysitting. I suppose it could be seen that way. Natalie wasn't especially amused when she got home. I'm sure she didn't tell me Joey wasn't allowed to drink milk. He should have told me himself, the little bugger. Anyhow, it proves babysitting is not my ideal career path, so I'm looking at some other options.

❦

Friday. 11am. Mel and I are stuffing around in her bedroom, trying on cheesy outfits. One of the things we have in common is that neither of us fits into a universe where glamour and beauty are the ultimate goals. We're the nerdy girls. Mel is skinny, but she has bad skin. She suffers from *acne vulgaris*, which sounds scary. It doesn't look that great, either. Her mother has dragged Mel to heaps of doctors, including a top dermatologist, and she's tried a zillion lotions and potions but her face and back are still covered with angry red eruptions. For a while it improved radically, but the goo she was using was nasty. If you dropped a blob on the carpet it bleached out all the colour. Seeing it's absorbed through the pores into the bloodstream, imagine what it does to your internal organs. Even the skin specialist advised her to only use it temporarily. Mel is a total greenie and she's a vegan. Because herbal remedies don't work and she's given up the toxic stuff her acne has returned, big-time.

Anyhow, the reason we're trying on these silly outfits is we're going to a New Year's Eve party and we have to go as fairies. Or something.

Magical Mystical Midsummer Party.
Dress in your finest laces and satins, fairy wings and goblin shoes.
Mocktails at 8pm. Frolic till Dawn
17 Harrington Crescent, Golden Bay
RSVP Poppy Marriot AKA starchic88@htmail.com

Poppy is not a nerdy girl. She's the queen of the beautiful people. Mel and I are only invited because Poppy's mother is Mel's mother's best friend.

'What does this look like, then?' I ask Mel. 'Really truly, I mean?'

We're working our way through the clothes Mel's sister left behind when she went to uni. I've squeezed myself into a red satin ball gown, which is very tight and horridly shiny but we're nearly at the bottom of the pile and I'm getting desperate.

'Really truly... not that great.'

I take a cautious look in the mirror.

'Not great! I look like a giant tomato.'

'It's not your fault, Georgie. It's the dress.'

'Maybe it would look okay on you,' I mutter. 'Give me a hand, will you? I'm stuck.' The skirt is caught around my bust and I can't get the stupid thing off. Mel tugs hard and sets me free.

'I've changed my mind, anyhow. I'm not going,' I add. Grumpiness has been sneaking up on me ever since we began trying on clothes. It's all very well to say that everyone is beautiful just the way they are, but the truth is that sometimes I feel fat and ugly and want to hide away forever.

'We are so going, Georgia. We told Poppy we would, and it's better than doing nothing on New Year's Eve.' Mel is trying to sound calm but she isn't doing so well. She hates it when we change plans. She's a Virgo. Not much flexibility, especially when her moon is in Scorpio.

'Whatever. You try the stupid dress on, then.'

'No way. It's dreadful. What about this black thing?'

'Nah. Was that from her Goth phase?' I chuck the leather mini-skirt back on the pile and flop down on the bed. Mel

things you either

doesn't bother answering. She checks out the final two items, a purple tie-dyed singlet and a ripped sarong, and chucks them on the reject pile. We lie on our backs and stare at the ceiling, a depressing sight because a leak has left a rusty stain resembling a brain tumour.

'The Hire Shop,' says Mel. 'Let's go there.'

'Yeah, I'm into it.' It can't be any worse than staring at the stain.

❤

At 4 o'clock we're sitting at a table in the sun outside Starfish, our favourite café.

'Not bad. Very good, actually,' I say.

'Yeah, yummy.'

We've ordered our usual. Two mango smoothies and a big plate of wedges. No animal has died in the making of these wedges, because they're made on the premises and fried in oil, not lard. Commercial wedges are a no-no because they're fried in animal fat. Mel checks everything thoroughly, believe me. Anyhow, because vegans don't eat dairy products I get all the sour cream, which is not a hardship. Mel likes the crispy wedges and I like the big wodgy ones. We're a good team.

'No, I meant the clothes. We aced it, baby.'

'True,' says Mel distractedly. She's testing the crunchiness of a medium-sized wedge by poking it with her finger. Our booty, in a motley collection of plastic bags, is stashed at our feet.

'The masks are brilliant. Once we glue — '

'Georgie,' Mel whispers. 'Look over there. No, don't look. I mean, don't make it obvious.' I turn my head in what I hope is an unobtrusive fashion.

'Toby, yeah?' I mutter, slurping on my smoothie.

'Shh, he's coming over.'

'The masks will look great once we glue the feathers on them,' I say loudly, trying to sound normal. Being around Toby always makes me feel awkward. He's the male equivalent of Poppy, good looking and popular, and always up with the latest trend. Today he's wearing a stripy hat resembling a tea-cosy. Both he and Mel are in the orchestra, and she has a drifty dreamy crush on him. I think he's a bit of a show pony but I never say so, just as Mel never admits to the crush. Toby plonks himself down and helps himself to our wedges, which is okay because we've eaten most of them and the remnants are getting cold.

'Masks?' he asks.

'Yeah. We're planning our outfits for Poppy's party.' It turns out Toby is going to the party, too, dressed as Puck. He still has his costume from *A Midsummer Night's Dream* last year.

'Mind if I smoke?' he enquires, taking out a packet of roll-your-owns.

'Care if we die?' I reply, but then I smile at him in a just-kidding way, for Mel's sake. To his credit, he shoves the packet back in his pocket.

'Gotta go, anyhow,' he says. 'Logan has the flu so I have to do an extra shift.'

'At Video World?'

'Yeah, why?'

'I'm looking for part-time work. Do they need more people?'

'I dunno. Maybe. You could come in and fill out the form. When they need someone they go through the forms and get people to come in for an interview. That's how I got my job.'

things you either

'Cool,' I say. 'Hey thanks, Toby.'

'See you Saturday.'

We watch him go. His pants are just the right amount of baggy. Even his lazy stroll seems calculatedly cool, but then he stuffs it up by fumbling for his rollies and dropping them. One minute he's outside the pizza shop, then he turns down the alley by the second-hand bookstore and is gone.

'Love that tea-cosy,' I smirk.

'You're such a mean-arse sometimes.' Mel's voice has a sharp note and she's looking at me in that disappointed way she has. At times like this our friendship is fragile. It's as if, all of a sudden, there's a great divide between us. Mel, the serene greenie on one side and Georgia, the bumbling idiot on the other.

'I'm sorry,' I say. 'It just that, I dunno, I always feel like a loser around people like him and Poppy. They're so on top of everything. So perfect, so normal, so...right.'

'Toby's not like that. He's just a person. You're not the only one with problems, you know.'

'What do you mean, problems?' Now I'm the one with an edge to my voice.

'Well, you don't have a dad...' She hesitates.

'And what else?' Go on, I'm thinking, go ahead and say it. A weight problem, that's what you mean, isn't it? Mel's head is bowed, her slender fingers are busy ripping her serviette to shreds. I'm about to say something dreadful when she looks up. Right at me. Her blue eyes are honest.

'This is crap, Georgia. Let's not fight. All I'm saying is that you aren't the only one who has stuff to deal with. Toby's got his share of weird shit.'

'Like what?'

'Like none of your business, that's what.'

'Do you fancy him?' There, I've finally said it. I take a slurp of my smoothie, a foolish slurp, because it's all gone.

'Maybe. Don't worry, it's nothing. I mean, he's Toby, right. He's never going to reciprocate or anything.'

'Why not?'

'You know why not. Because of my skin. Come on, let's get going or we're going to miss the bus.'

tiaras and tears

New Year's Eve. Mel's parents are going to a big Latin Fiesta so she'll be sleeping at my house. We've gone over and over our party plans. Mel will get dropped off around 6 o'clock, which gives us ages to get ready. Mum will drop us at Poppy's and pick us up at 12.30. I try to make her come later, say 2 am, but she won't budge. She's already given me her *Alcohol is Evil* lecture, which seems rather hypocritical since her fridge is crammed with champagne and beer. She also attempts a repeat performance of her embarrassing *Sex is for Later* talk, but I pretend I have to go to the toilet and stay in there for ages reading *Rolling Stone*. By the time I come out she's forgotten about me and is wandering around the garden picking roses. She's having a little party herself: Joy and Kev and a few other people are coming over, so we spend the afternoon preparing.

When it's tidied and tizzied up, our house has a nice feel. I like the way the light shines through the stained glass on the front door, making rainbow diamonds down the hall. From the kitchen window you see the garden: a tangled tropical world of bougainvillea and bamboo. We listen to reggae, the only music we both like. Bob Marley is good

things you either

music to cook to. Mum puts on her flowery apron and makes an amazing dessert called Summer Clouds, using strawberries, raspberries, egg whites, sugar and large amounts of cream. I marinate chicken wings in honey and soya sauce, and cycle to the shops to buy ciabatta bread. When Mel turns up, late and laden with bags, we sit in the garden for afternoon tea. Coffee for me and Mum, ginger tea for Mel. Frangipani fragrance scents the dusky air. I'm looking forward to the party. It's New Year's Eve, a time of new beginnings. Anything might happen.

'I'm dying to see your outfits,' Mum tells Mel. 'Georgia has been very mysterious about what you're wearing. She won't tell me, just keeps coming in and borrowing scarves and things.'

'Yeah, well, patience is a virtue, Mumsie. Come on, Mel. Let's get ready.'

We make our grand entrance just after eight. We've glued and sewed and primped and polished and painted, all to the latest Natural Affinity CD, *Flip,* played top volume. We're as ready as we're ever going to be. We look pretty fine. I don't even feel fat, I just feel curvy.

'Oh wow. You guys look fantastic. Those masks are wonderful.' It's a buzz to see Mum so delighted by us. Sometimes mothers pretend things but this is for real.

'We're not sure who we are though. Mel reckons we're ragged fairies from the underworld but I think we look more like witches.'

'Well, you look like glory goddesses to me. Come into the garden, I'll get my camera and take a picture.'

Mel doesn't usually let anyone take her photograph, but she doesn't protest. We adjust our black lace dresses so they fit just right and slinky, drape our flimsy scarves for the sultriest effect. Our lips are blood red, our eyes kohl dark, our faces powder pale. We've decorated our gilded cardboard masks with peacock feathers and tiny silk roses. We've sprayed ourselves with Mum's *Je Reviens* perfume, which smells like sexy flowers. We're ready to rock.

❦

Mel and me, standing beside the sparkly mosaic bird bath, trying to look regal, trying not to giggle.

'Say cheese, say sex, say Vegemite,' says Mum.

'Sexy Vegemite!' we yell. Snap. World's our oyster, sky's the limit, best of friends. Arms around each other. Faces alive with sparkle and grin.

But then, out of the blue, comes a weird thought. *One day all this will just be a memory.* A shiver runs down my spine, a little melancholy breeze.

'Come on,' I say, in a voice loud and bright, to scare away the ghosts. 'We've got a party to go to.'

❦

Poppy's house isn't exactly buzzing when we arrive. No one's there except Eva, Poppy's best friend. She opens the door to greet us, wearing a tiara and a very short dress decorated with green crepe paper leaves.

'Hi Georgie. Hi Mel.' Eva is one of my least favourite people. She lacks Poppy's charm. In fact, a person with less dignity than *moi* might refer to her as a snooty bitch.

'Come on in. Great you could make it. Do you want a Bloodless Mary or a Peachy Dream?' Eva has spent years perfecting her bored tone. It's almost, but not quite, a sneer. She uses it when teachers ask why she hasn't done her homework, but it doesn't seem quite as amusing now she's

things you either

using it on us. I raise my eyebrows in what I hope is a droll manner. I have no idea what she's on about.

'Tomato juice with bitters, or a peach smoothie?' she explains.

'Peach thing,' I blurt, at the same time Mel replies, 'I'll try the Bloodless Mary.' Then we nearly trip over each other following Eva down the hall. I give Mel a look. *What the hell are we doing here can we please go home?* But she turns her head away like an elegant swan, pretending I don't exist.

I must admit the party decorations are cool. Silver and gold streamers, white balloons, tubs of white lilies. Eva pours our drinks from shiny cocktail shakers. Mel sits in a bean bag and I plonk myself on the couch, next to the sushi platter.

'Poppy won't be long. She's in her room. There's a major crisis.'

'What's up?' asks Mel politely.

'Logan might not be coming. I don't know the full story. They're texting each other as we speak.'

'How horrendous,' I say. Eva gives me a filthy look. I beam her a smile and pop a whole sushi in my mouth to gross her out. It takes a bit of chewing but the effort is worth it. Eva is shocked but pretends to ignore me and turns to Mel.

'I've got some vodka. Want some?'

'Nah, we're shweet,' I say cheerfully, even though she wasn't speaking to me. I love saying shweet. It's really annoying if you do it often enough. I do it all the time in class. It's classic.

I offer the sushi platter to Mel, who inspects it for pieces of sea creature. Finally she manages to find an avocado/

carrot/cucumber number to her liking, and takes a delicate bite.

'Fusion cooking.' I say brightly. 'So happening. So very, very now.' It seems I'm way too much fun for Eva.

'Back soon,' she says as she hastens from the room.

'Shweet,' I call after her. 'Love your toenails!'

'What is that winsome shade of green?' I say, once Eva's safely out of earshot. 'Revlon's Noxious Nile? Gruesome Green, by Maybelline?'

'Georgia! Get a goddamn grip!'

'Why, Mel? Will I have to go home if I'm naughty?'

We sit silently and sulk.

❦

'So, New Year,' I say after a while, getting bored. 'The year collapses into itself, then rises fresh and new. A time of magic and opportunity.' Mel regards me suspiciously, not sure if I'm taking the micky.

'I prefer the Chinese system,' she says, giving me the benefit of the doubt. I'm glad. I've learned it's not wise to push Mel too hard. She stays calm up to a certain point, then shuts down entirely and frosts me out for ages. Once it took me a very painful fortnight to crawl back into her good books, but that's another story.

'What sign are you again, in Chinese astrology?' I ask.

'Rabbit.'

'Oh, that's right. I'm a Dragon. We're charming, intelligent and tenacious. Mum's a Pig, which she finds embarrassing.'

'Actually pigs are good. They like luxury, and making other people happy.'

'Yeah, well, that sounds like my mum. So, what are Rabbits all about?'

32

things you either

'Sensitive. Loyal to family and friends. Delicate constitutions. We get sick easily, apparently.'

'Do you think that fits you?'

'Kind of. There's different sorts of rabbit, it depends on your birth year. I'm a Fire Rabbit, not an Earth Rabbit. If you're really into astrology, you can combine the two systems, Chinese and Western. A Capricorn Rabbit is different to a Pisces Rabbit, for example.'

'Do you believe in it, Mello?'

'Yeah. Well, only kind of.' She grins at me. Whew. We're friends again.

'What year are we in now, anyhow?'

'The Horse, but in February it'll be the Year of the Goat.'

'All righty, then. Here's to The Year of the Goat! To things that start with G. To gremlins, geese and grandmothers.'

'Gargoyles.'

'Graveyards.'

'Grasshoppers.'

'God, where is everybody? This is getting weird.'

As if on cue, we hear a rumble of laughter and a tumble of loud knocking outside the front door. Poppy rushes downstairs, and Eva reappears too, clutching a small bottle of vodka.

'Leave a few, won't you,' she snarls at me, grabbing a piece of sushi. She looks a bit…ruffled. I refrain from saying, 'Ya, Frau Eva. I alvays obey ze Sushi Police.' Eva is scary enough sober, but she's not sober now. She almost topples onto Mel as she stashes her bottle behind the bean bag.

🍷

Enter the party animals. The chosen ones from Year Ten at Golden Bay High, posing and carrying on big time. Logan has decided to show. Ben and Jack too. Toby. Caris and Emma. Hannah and Finn. Tania and Nick. Carly. Here's the embarrassing part. Most of them haven't made much effort with their outfits. Some, let's be honest, haven't made any at all. I feel overdressed and stupid, but there's nowhere to run and no place to hide.

❤

Poppy looks great, as always. Her hair has red streaks, and is pinned up in elaborate whirly bits like angel's ringlets. She's wearing a fairy costume of wafty dress and sparkly wings. Toby matches Eva in her leafy green with his emerald Puck costume: perky cap, matching tunic and tights. Caris and Emma look exactly as they always do: boring pastel girly clothes and lots of make-up. Tania looks good. Her turquoise dress is nothing special but her shoes are magical: pointy toes and golden embroidery, the shoes of a Turkish princess. Nick is draped in a sheet with a belt around it, like a kid of five who's supposed to be one of the three wise men in the Christmas concert but whose Mum didn't get around to making him a proper costume. At least he doesn't have a tea towel on his head and at least he made some effort. Not like Logan, Ben and Jack, in their ultra-baggy jeans and expensive skate logo t-shirts. Hannah and Finn are into the semi-Goth thing, so they're just themselves, dressed in black. Which leaves Carly, the only girl in our year who's fatter than me. She's wearing a beaded cardigan, wide-legged jeans, and the forced smile of someone who likes parties as much as I do.

❤

things you either

Here's the thing.

The party was not fun. Eva got drunker and drunker. She kept playing shite bubble-gum pop, then Logan took over and played poor quality rap. No one danced, except Caris and Emma, the show-offs. Someone should tell them that disco died. I scoured the entire music selection but couldn't find one Natural Affinity CD. Mel and Toby sat outside under a tree for most of the night engrossed in intimate conversation. I left them to it, which took great self restraint. Mel, you owe me. Hannah flirted with Jack, which was weird, but then she's weird, so it makes sense. I tried talking to Finn, but he was so stoned I couldn't get any sense out of him. Adrian and a few other guys turned up. Adrian's in my Media Studies class and we compared notes on our assignment about marketing and youth culture. He didn't stay long. He and his crew had another party to go to. I hid in the study for ages, looking at books, but got so bored that in desperation I snuck a few slurps of Eva's vodka, thinking no one was watching me. Unfortunately I got sprung. Eva yelled at me incredibly loudly, which was ghastly. I won't repeat her exact words. Too mortifying. Everyone stared at me as if I was pitiful. Perhaps I am.

So I executed an old manoeuvre, but one that works for me. I hid out in the kitchen and ate. Quite a bit. Felt sick. Mel came in to get a drink of water and remarked that cheesecake is one of the unhealthiest things you can eat. Thanks Mel. Sat on front step and wished I was dead for eleven minutes. Made up small rhyming verse trashing Eva. Sang it loudly. Felt marginally better. Went for a walk down the street and stole some roses. Ripped heads off roses. Threw petals in the air, all over myself, like a wedding. Came back and sat on front step for eleven years.

Somewhere between now and infinity Eva came out and chundered on the lawn. I tried to show sympathy. Truly, I did. I got her a damp cloth and a towel and helped her get cleaned up. To her credit Eva was drunkenly apologetic but she smelled of sick so I didn't linger. Walked down street again but was discouraged by the ferocious barking of a huge German Shepherd. Took up my position on the front step once more. By now it was 11.45pm. Yay. Almost time to go home. At midnight Logan found a radio station that played *Auld Lang Syne*. We all joined hands and said Happy New Year, then milled around feeling foolish while Poppy made coffee. I joined Mel and Toby in the garden. They tried to include me in their discussion about global warming but I began to doze off. Am glad Mum didn't agree to a 2am pick-up, though I'll never admit it.

One good thing happened at the party. Just as we were leaving, Toby told me that a guy got fired from Video World for letting his friend take videos home for free. This means there might be a position vacant. I'm going to head on down tomorrow afternoon, when they open, to see if I can get myself some work.

❣

'Happy New Year, Mama.'

'Happy New Year, Georgie. Happy New Year, Mel. How was the party, darling?'

'It was good. Neat food. Great decorations.'

'Were your outfits a hit?'

'Yeah, everybody loved them.'

Sometimes you just have to lie.

❣

things you either

Mel sits in the front seat, talking to Mum. I sit in the back and lean out the window, enjoying the breeze on my face, pretending I'm in New York or somewhere fabulous. I hope it's going to be a good year. A year of parties that aren't boring. A year of mystery and delight. Tra la la.

'What are you thinking, *chica*?' Mum asks, trying to include me in the conversation. She learned a little Spanish when she went to South America with my father, a million years ago, when they were young. I try to visualise my father but I can't remember his face. Mum's voice sounds far away.

'I'm pretending I'm somewhere fabulous.'

There's a pregnant pause. I can sense what's coming — she's going to go all spiritual on me. She does it on special occasions, like birthdays and like, well, like now. Sometimes I wish she hadn't been to all those retreats. Her wisdom is not always my wisdom.

'What's the matter with the here and now? Isn't this moment perfect just as it is?'

'Mmm,' I murmur. I don't have the strength to discuss it tonight. If I did, I'd tell her the truth, which is that no, right now is not fabulous at all. I don't have a father. I don't have a boyfriend. I don't have a life. No one at the party felt I was worth talking to. Mel would rather hang out with Toby than with me. I spent fifteen bucks hiring a black lace dress which no one even complimented me on. (Only Eva, who didn't mean it, and my mother, which doesn't count.) Even worse, I ripped a hole in the stupid hem when I was nicking roses, so I'll probably lose my deposit as well. Now my bank balance is Way Messed Up and I will never get to see Jakob. He'll never fall in love with me, his one true fan and soulmate, when he notices me sitting in the front row of the concert. To complete this crappy state of affairs, I feel nauseous, for which I can only blame myself. So, no. Life is not fabulous. In fact, it is seriously stuffed.

❦

When we get home nearly everyone has left. Penny, Mum's closest friend, is on her way out the door with Roxanne, her poodle, tucked under her arm. We stop to admire Roxanne's party outfit. Penny is a textile artist who makes gorgeous things. The little dog's jacket is brilliant. Purple crepe with a fake leopard-skin collar and nifty Velcro tabs. It fits perfectly. Roxanne has a classier wardrobe than most humans.

'*Ciao*, darling,' Penny says, heading unsteadily down the path. 'I did a few dishes. Superb party. I'll call you soon.'

The house has the After Party Blues. Chewed olive pips dot the browning remains of the guacamole. Bottles huddle at the back door; a broken glass smudged with lipstick sits lonely on the bench. But the most mournful thing of all is Joy, sitting at the kitchen table scooping the remnants of the creamy berry pudding out of the bowl with her finger.

'He's gone. He's gone and I don't blame him.' She wipes froth off her chin, licks her sticky fingers. 'This is delicious, Annie. You're a great cook. I can't cook. But I've made a shit-and-mustard sandwich of my life. You betcha... I'll have to stay the night,' she continues, slurring her words. 'I might have to shift in and live here forever. Georgia won't like that. She doesn't like me. Nobody likes me.'

This is Very Very Weird. My uptight to-the-point-of-frozen-solid aunt is drunk. Pissed as a pudding, as the saying goes. Mum takes charge, although she looks somewhat alarmed.

38

things you either

'Come on, Joy. Don't be silly. Everybody likes you. And of course you can stay the night, you can sleep on the divan in my study.'

'I want some more champagne. I deserve some more champagne. Come on Annie, let's get sloshed.'

My aunt has firm views on everything. She is particularly opposed to what she calls 'bad language'. I don't think I've even heard her say 'damn' before now, which makes tonight's outburst very scary.

'You've had enough champagne tonight, darling. Why don't we have a cup of tea instead.' Mum motions me and Mel to go upstairs to bed.

'I hate him,' Joy suddenly blurts out. 'But I love him as well.' She starts sobbing, great big weepy gulps. More frantic waving from Mum. Mel and I mumble our goodnights and scoot.

I'd like to hang about on the stairs and eavesdrop, but I'm too exhausted. I drag the spare mattress from under my bed while Mel puts on her green pyjamas. I want to forget about cleaning my teeth and taking off my make-up. I want to forget about everything: disappointing parties, ripped hems and drunk aunties. Mel, however, insists we cleanse our faces with organic cucumber goo, which smells nothing like cucumbers. Once we are tucked up in our beds, eyes closed, sleepy and cosy in the darkness, she says a strange thing.

'What does it taste like?'

'What does what taste like?'

'Fish. The fish in sushi.'

'It tastes good. Salty and chewy and fishy.'

'I've started dreaming about it. About fish.'

'Why don't you eat some then?'

'I don't want to eat living things.'

'Vegetables are living and you eat them.'

We've had this exact conversation at least six times before. The next bit goes like this: Mel says, 'Everyone draws a line somewhere. You choose not to eat rats or cockroaches, I choose not to eat anything with eyes.' Then I say, 'Potatoes have eyes.' Then we both laugh or else we both get pissed off with each other, depending on our mood. Tonight we're so tired we don't bother to do anything, we just roll over and go to sleep. I dream I'm being chased by a giant oily sushi, which turns into a ferocious German Shepherd who turns into Aunty Joy, who says I'm not allowed to go to the Natural Affinity concert until I've cleaned her entire house using a tiny lace handkerchief. A dream from which I am very glad to wake, around noon on New Year's Day.

new beginnings

Mel is nowhere to be seen. I stumble downstairs, find a note on the bench.

> *Gone for a walk in the Botanical Gardens with Joy.*
> *Don't eat the smoked salmon. Back later. xoxoxo Mum*

I spy Mel, in her green pyjamas, doing Tai Chi down by the lemon tree. She looks graceful, like a stork, about to fly away. I make food: buttery raisin toast for me, fruit salad sprinkled with nuts for Mel, and strong coffee. We discuss the party in a desultory manner. We agree that Poppy rocks, Logan sucks, Eva totally sucks, Caris and Emma will always suck. Furthermore, we note that Hannah and Finn have split up, Tania's shoes are fab and Nick's costume was

things you either

seriously sad. Then we get dressed because it's time for Mel's dad to pick her up.

After Mel has gone I turn on my computer and start to write a CV in order to have something to impress them with at Video World. I hunt down a sample one on the internet but it's hard when you haven't had any jobs, so I fudge it a bit.

NAME   Georgia Amy Reeves
ADDRESS   79 Russell Street
                Golden Bay PLANET WEIRD
PHONE   9543 7792
DATE OF BIRTH   April 7th 1988

WORK HISTORY
Founder of the Modernist movement 1937
Cauliflower Farmer — 1991-1992
Brain Surgeon — 1992-2001

CURRENT EMPLOYMENT
Natural Affinity groupie
Volunteer for Market Research into
Recreational Drugs

OTHER INFORMATION:
Georgia is extraordinarily delightful
in every way. There's nothing this
girl can't achieve, given the right
circumstances and a shit-load of money.
Georgia is intelligent, intuitive,
insightful and illustrious. She has
promised to give up shoplifting and
start wearing deodorant. Georgia is an

hate or love   41

Aries Earth Dragon who believes in girl
power and mashed potatoes. I recommend
her to you highly, unless you are
after someone who knows how to do
electrolysis, in which case, forget it.

EDUCATIONAL QUALIFICATIONS:
Msc, ABC, Dip Ed, Rhu.Barb.
Advanced Diploma in Genuine Foul-
Mouthed Chickiedom from the University
of Hogwarts.
Diploma of Excellence from the School
of Hard Knocks.

REFEREES:
The Tooth Fairy, God, Santa Claus.

Hmm, not bad. I'd hire me, for sure.

I print out a copy, decorate it with hibiscus flowers, then take it downstairs and stick it to the fridge door with star magnets. I sneak some smoked salmon, cunningly rearranging the slices so you can't tell. My scrap of salmon looks rather lonely on the plate so I add olives and cold garlic bread. I pretend it's my lunch, but since it's only been an hour since breakfast even I am not fully convinced. I turn on the telly, decide not to watch golf or cartoons, then go upstairs to seek out an outfit which will make me appear reliable and intelligent. Nothing looks right. Nothing fits properly, except my big floppy Indian dress that I got in the 50 cent bin at an op shop. Perhaps I could wear the black lace party dress? Nah, perhaps not.

᭡

things you either

I wish Mum and Auntie Joy would come home so I'd have someone to talk to, which is seriously desperate. I scrounge around looking for the Tilt CD Mel gave me for Christmas and finally retrieve it from under my bed, along with the white bra I lost months ago. In the dusty land of lost things I also discover the yellow satin journal. I haul it out and stare at it blankly for a while. I drag my school backpack out of the wardrobe, because somewhere in there, maybe, is my Personal Portfolio, which contains my school marks and some other stuff that might help me score a job. This turns into a Terrible Huge Saga because everything falls out and my folders and notes end up scattered all over the floor. I begin shoving them into my backpack in a haphazard fashion, then I change my mind. Now is as good a time as any to sort the whole lot out, I guess.

❤

GEORGIA'S Impressive 8 POINT Plan

1. Chuck out all unwanted written material. Make important decision that there is no need to keep a piece of paper on which is scrawled the following:

> CARIS loves JACK
> JACK loves EMMA
> EMMA loves LOGAN
> LOGAN loves POPPY
> POPPY loves DaiSies!$#@%&*!!!

I have no idea who wrote these profound words. Poppy perhaps? But how did they get in amongst my Biology notes? This must remain one of the unsolved mysteries of the universe. I have work to do.

2. Empty all my loose leaf files, label them BY SUBJECT

with my big black permanent marker, then put them away VERY NEATLY in bottom desk drawer.

3. Put empty files back in school backpack.
4. Feel so virtuous it's scary. Is this how I'm to spend the new year, as St Georgia, patron saint of the tidy people?
5. Organise my fluffy purple pencil case. Throw away broken biro, dried-up felt pens, dodgy highlighter that leaks, stub of ink-stained eraser, complete with toothmarks.
6. Make note of stationery requirements, which are many, including new gel pens, glittery pens, purple highlighter, three good black pens, red pen, decent ruler, etc.
7. Chuck away fossilised mandarin, dead elastic band and four scrumpled tissues.
8. Open window. Hold bag upside down out the window & bang on it so fluff and crud fall out.

Exhausted by my dazzling efforts, I snuggle down in bed and talk to Jakob about music, our favourite topic. As ever he is silent. He's a fine listener, though.

❦

'Where have you been? It's nearly 3 o'clock,' I demand, when Mum finally returns.

'We went for a walk in the Botanical Gardens. I told you in my note. The hot house is magical, all those beautiful orchids and fuchsias. Then I took Joy home and stayed for coffee. Didn't realise it was so late, though. Have you had lunch?'

'Sort of. What's up with Joy and Kevin, anyhow?'

'I'm starving. I'm going to have a smoked salmon bagel. Want one?'

things you either

'Yeah, yummy.' I'm not actually hungry but I don't want to let on, in case she figures out that I raided the salmon. My mother may think she's successfully avoided answering my question but she hasn't. 'So what's the deal? I've never seen Aunty Joy like that before.'

'It's complicated, Georgie. They're having a few problems right now. I probably shouldn't go into it.'

'Yeah, whatever,' I say grumpily. The whole world is built of secrets. None of them mine. 'How come she's acting so nuts, anyhow? She's always so uptight and controlling, then suddenly she becomes a drunken drama queen. She's scary, like a dark river, murky and dangerous.'

'Ours wasn't an easy family, you know. Nana and her depression, three kids so close together in age packed into a small house, never having enough money. Joy was damaged by it, I suppose.'

'But you're normal, more or less.'

'I'll take that as a compliment.' Mum smiles, then looks pensive.

'People respond to things in different ways, you know. Joy was always the sensitive one. She was such a gentle little kid. She'd sit under the wisteria for ages, making peg dolls with happy faces and poppy petal skirts. She tucked insects in matchboxes for pets and named our bantam hens cheerful things like Tulip and Honeypot. Joy always tried to create calmness in the midst of chaos. The very opposite of Sooze, who was wild and tried to break out, right from the start. The first time she left home she was only four. She took off on her tricycle, with a little wicker basket of comics; been running away from things ever since. As for me, I was just…I don't know, I was just me. Somewhere in between. Maybe it's our karma.'

'What is karma, anyhow? I've never quite got that.'

'Well, actions have cause and effects. Karma means you arrive in this life bringing the results of past lives.'

'Do you believe in it?' My mother doesn't usually talk about this sort of stuff. She just goes off on her retreats and comes home very serene, which lasts a week or so.

'Some mysteries can't be explained. Things just unfold, brightness and shadow, difficulty and delight. I believe in taking responsibility for your actions, though. Even if we only have one life, we reap what we sow.'

'That makes sense.'

'So, what have you been up to?'

'I started to write a CV to take down to Video World. Toby said there might be a job going, but the CV is a disaster, and I've got nothing to wear.'

'What's the matter with what you've got on?'

'Yeah, right,' I say, looking down at my fat thighs. 'I look so budget in this.'

'You look fine to me. Do you want my help with the CV?'

'Nah, I sorted out all my school stuff and unearthed my Personal Portfolio, which has my grades in it, and what clubs I'm in, and how I won the English competition and the Citizenship Award.'

'Sounds good. Don't forget to tell them about your work experience at the Hilton. And babysitting. And the Penny thingy.'

'Might leave out the babysitting. Can't use Natalie as a reference, she'll tell them I poisoned her snotty little rug rat. What do you mean, tell them about Penny?'

'You know, when you helped advertise her art workshop by taking leaflets around to libraries and community notice-boards.'

'I can't count *that*, Mum.'

'Course you can. She paid you, so it was a job. Casual work as a promotions assistant. They won't know that the woman you did it for happens to be your mother's best friend. Most resumes are heavily padded with half truths such as these.'

'If you say so. Can I borrow the necklace? I'll wear these jeans and my black shirt, but I need a bit of sparkle.'

'As long as you don't lose it.'

'I'm so glad you said that. I was planning on throwing it into a hydrangea bed, or leaving it in a rubbish skip, just to annoy you.'

'Georgia!'

I poke out my tongue at her.

'I'll get the necklace. Do you need a ride to Video World?'

'Nah, I'll ride my bike. I'm going over to Mel's after that to say goodbye. We arranged it this morning. Mel has to pack. She's going to the beach tomorrow, for two weeks. I'll be home for tea though.'

❦

I look like a gothic whale in my black jeans and black shirt. Mum's chunky crystal necklace only serves to make me resemble a whale with good taste in jewellery. By the time I get to Video World it's five o'clock, and I'm all sweaty. When I remove my helmet my hair's stuck to my forehead. I lock my bike out of sight, on the far side of the car park, and lurk around for ages, trying to psyche myself into entering the store. Quite a few customers are coming and going, which strikes me as sad. Surely there are better things to do on a sunny summer's afternoon than watch

Arnold Schwarzenegger kick arse, especially as it's the first day of a new year.

'What's the worst thing that can happen?' I ask myself. This is a possibly daft idea that I read in a self-help book. Once you've worked out the worst outcome of your current predicament you tell yourself that if *that* happened, you could handle it. Then you go for it. Feel the fear and do it anyway. Hmmm.

Okay, here goes. The worst thing that could happen is that they won't give me a job. I could handle that, I guess. Except that I want the stupid job really really badly. Heaps of young funky film-makers work in video shops. It's a key feature of my Famous Film-Maker Fantasy, which goes like this: Get the video store job. Rent a squalid old house and live there, with two stoned university students and a cat called Bonk. Somehow survive destitution, existing on baked beans and dreams. Manage to scrape together the cash to make a low-budget feature film, a stunning first effort that takes the world by storm. My pic gets a standing ovation at the Toronto Film Festival and is picked up by Miramax. I sell out to Hollywood. Become extremely rich but not very happy. Have a brief flirtation with cocaine, which gradually starts to take me down, so I run away to Berlin where I have a doomed love affair with a Czech violin player and his exquisite young wife. Broken-hearted, I return to drugs and do many dreadful things but eventually rise from the dark ashes of my own madness to become a tranquil yoga practitioner and the best photographer in the whole world.

I can embroider this one for hours. However, I don't have hours, because I told Mel I'd be at her place at four thirty, so I'm already running late.

Furthermore, I know in my heart that the worst thing

things you either

that could happen is much more dreadful than not getting the job. The guy behind the counter could slowly look me up and down, take a quick glance at my Personal Portfolio, chuck it in the bin, and then dismiss me with the following:

'Sure. There's a cool job going. Eleven dollars an hour and free videos. Thursday and Friday evenings from four till nine, and all day Saturday. The occasional public holiday, for which you get paid extra. But you're nothing but a slobby blubbery person, so we won't be giving the job to *you*. In fact, we don't even like having you in our shop. You're scaring the customers, so shove off.'

All right, the chances of this are slim, I realise, then giggle, out loud and somewhat hysterically, at the irony of the word slim in this particular context. Then I go in.

❤

The first person I see is Toby. He's not wearing his tea-cosy hat; in fact he's sporting a new haircut which must have been hidden last night under his green cap. This hairstyle is seriously sick. Close-cropped short back and sides, the top bit longer and nicely gelled up into a stylishly tousled mess. I gotta admit, Mel, I can see the attraction.

Toby grins at me. 'Hey, Georgia. Good timing. Stuart's out the back, he's the guy who hires and fires. I'll go and see if he's free.' So far, so good.

Stuart is thirty-something, kind of grungy, with thinning hair. His skin is pale, and best of all, he's overweight. He looks like a big friendly slug that spends its life alone, indoors, watching vids and eating sleazy greasy junk food. Yay, I smile to myself. There's no way he'll be against lardy-arse people, seeing he is one.

'So. Georgia, is it? Toby says you're looking for work?'

'Yep.' That was dumb. I should have said 'Yes' in a posh voice, to demonstrate my smooth customer skills, but old Stu doesn't seem to have noticed.

'Come on then. Let's go out the back and I'll ask you a few questions.'

The lunch room is rank. Grotty coffee cups, ciggie butts, dead air. I move some magazines off a chair and sit down, clearing a space for my portfolio by shifting an ancient sausage roll to one side.

'Tell me about your work history, Georgia.'

'Um, right. Well, I've done *heaps* of babysitting, and I did my Year Ten work experience at the Hilton.'

'In what capacity?'

'I helped set up the function room, cleared restaurant tables and worked in the kitchen.'

'Had any cash register experience?'

'Not really. I had another job though, helping promote an art course.' Even to me, this sounds lame.

'Have you done any work involving customer service?'

'No, but I'm very reliable. Here's my Personal Portfolio, if you'd like to have a look?'

'Sure,' he replies, so I reach for my folder. Oops. I went too close to the sausage roll. That wasn't the look I was aiming for. There's a smear of congealed tomato sauce on my CV. I hand it over, smear and all.

'I see you're in the drama club. I liked drama when I was at school.'

'Yeah, it's fun.' God, I sound pathetic. I'm starting to panic.

'Okay, let's test your Maths. Have a crack at these. I'll be back in a minute.'

Maths is not my forte but I do the best I can. The questions are quite hard and seem to have no relevance to

things you either

the job. How come I need to be able to do fractions to hand over two videos and a Violet Crumble? I thought the cash register did the hard stuff. I'm only half way through when Stuart returns, yakking on his mobile. He gestures me to give him back the sheet, and takes a quick distracted squiz.

'All righty, yeah. Okay then, later, man. Cheers, man. Later.' One conversation over, and another one about to bite the dust.

'Right, Georgia. Thanks for coming in. I have a few other people to interview but I'll be in touch, okay?'

'Sure,' I say meekly. 'Shall I write my details on the Maths sheet?'

'What? Yeah, good plan.'

I scrawl my name, address and phone number. I should have written it neatly, but who cares? He'll never call, and we both know it.

'Bye, then. Thanks. I'm sure I could be a useful part of your team,' I say unconvincingly. Stuart busies himself with some forms so I make my own way out. Toby is serving a customer. I give him a tiny wave and get out of there.

I shove on my stupid helmet, hop on my bike and pedal away as fast as I can. When I reach the park near the river, I plonk myself down under a shady tree and cry.

This is what Eva said to me at the party.

Get yourself a life, you fat loser.

lonely days without mel

Saying goodbye to Mel is hard. She's in drifty mode, trying on clothes and removing a stain from her Mambo hat. She rabbits on about Tom and Jodie Ferrier. She's hung out with the twins every summer since before she was born, practically. I met them a couple of years ago and found them dreary. Tom stared at my boobs, and Jodie was a boring people-pleaser. Or perhaps I just wanted Mel to myself. I didn't like going to the Ferriers' swanky beach house every evening to play cheesy board games. The parents got trashed on gin and tonic and forgot to make us any dinner.

'What about this?' Mel asks.

'Not bad.' Mel looks good in pretty much anything though I'm wondering if I should mention that the purple muslin dress is very see-through. You can see her skinny legs and white undies quite clearly, especially when she stands in the doorway. Quite sexy, actually, but probably not the effect she's after. Not with sleazy old Tom around, anyhow.

'You can see through it a bit, though,' I mumble, not sure if I'm being a noble friend or a mean-arse.

'Really? Oh well, never mind, I'll only be wearing it on the beach, anyhow.'

'True. Hey, I went to Video World, Toby was there. He's got this seriously cool new haircut.'

'I know. He showed me last night. It cost heaps. He had it done by the pierced girl at Headworxx. So how did the job thingy go?'

'Pretty crap. They won't give me any work, that's for sure.'

'Why not? You could do it standing on your head.'

'Yeah, well, you and I know that, but the boss man wasn't easy to convince. I don't have any till experience and I didn't get far with the Maths test. I came across very poorly indeed, as they say.'

'I bet you didn't, Georgia. You always say how crap you did in exams and then you ace it.'

things you either

'True. But sadly, this time I really did do crap. Just call me the girl who cried crap too often. Anyhow, gotta go. It's getting dark and my bike light is broken.'

'Don't you want to stay for tea? Dad could help sort out your bike light if you like.'

'Nah, better not. I told Mum I'd be home for dinner. Thanks though. Have a great time at the beach. I'll miss you.'

'Me too.'

'Bring me a starfish.'

'I'll bring you three, and a seahorse.'

'Choice.'

'See ya, Georgie.'

★

When I get home, Mum is in the bath listening to Elgar. I put on The Waifs instead, ignoring her protest. We make a haphazard meal of the remains of the party food, followed by a mango each. Mum doesn't interrupt as I tell her about the dreadful job interview. She then gives me a pep talk about *How I am beautiful, wonderful and terrific.* I wish I didn't need her to prop me up, but I do feel better.

'About Joy and Kevin,' Mum says, flossing shreds of mango from between her teeth.

'Yeah?'

'They should never have got married. Joy thought she was pregnant, so good old Kevin did the right thing and asked her. Then it turned out she wasn't pregnant, but the wedding plans were in motion, so they went ahead with it. Gilda was conceived almost straight away. Joy and Kev stuck with it and tried to make it work, but somehow it never quite did.'

'It sounds as if it should have been a starter marriage.'

'What on earth is that?'

'I read about them in that magazine Gilda left behind. Hang on, I'll find it. Here we go. "A starter marriage is a short lived first marriage that ends in divorce, with no children, no property and no regrets."'

'Mmm,' says Mum. 'Well, Joy and Kevin have been together so long that I can't imagine them apart, but the way things are they aren't going to last much longer.'

'Are they having a major meltdown?'

'That's one way of putting it. I'm not even sure what to think about it. No point carrying on if it's too awful, but how tragic if it all comes down to dust.'

I glance at Mum. She looks so sad. Without missing a beat, she changes the subject. 'Want to watch a video?'

'What've we got?'

'Not much. That spy movie, and a gardening show.'

'Nah, I'll pass.'

'Okay. Oh, I had a look at the lace dress and I mended the rip. The hire shop won't even know.'

'Hey thanks. You're the best, Mum.'

♥

I wander up to my room and stare out the window for ages, then I take out the yellow journal and start writing.

Things I wish I hadn't done at the party
 Arrived so early
 Dressed up flamboyantly
 Eaten half a plate of sushi
 Refused to mix with people
 Stolen Eva's vodka
 Scoffed too much cheesecake
 Felt so lonely

things you either

things i love by Georgia

Clothing:	*The gold Indian shawl Mum gave me last Christmas*
Footwear:	*My black brocade slippers*
Food:	*Toasted ham & cheese sandwiches*
Book:	*Catherine, Called Birdy by Karen Cushman*
Films:	*Rocky Horror Picture Show, I Capture the Castle, Amelie*
Animal:	*Dragon*
Beverage:	*Mango yoghurt smoothie*
Hobby:	*Daydreaming about Jakob*
Bird:	*Penguin, rainbow lorikeet*
Flower:	*Peonies, jasmine, frangipani, roses*
Planet:	*Mars*
Jewel:	*Ruby, turquoise, amethyst, emerald*
Smell:	*Coffee, tea rose perfume, fried onions*
Car:	*Volkswagen*
Dog:	*Basset hound*

wordz that it iz hard to spel

genious
haemaroyds
tommorrow
Hawaiiaii
miscelanneaous
mischieeevious
psykologist
neice
sandwhiches
embrodiery
eigthhh (8th!)

Lists are good. When I did my big clean out I found my old Lit notes, about autobiographical writing and Sei Shonagon, a famous diarist. She was a lady-in-waiting for the Empress Sadako in the last decade of the 10th century and wrote amazing lists in her Pillow Book, which became an important record of life at that time. She listed the things that gladdened her heart, as well as depressing things and puzzling things. She actually made some very odd lists, such as things that should never be painted, and things that looked better from the front than from behind, like embroidery (and Carly).

Anyhow, since I am bored beyond belief and must find a new hobby to replace frying cheese sandwiches in butter, I have decided use the yellow satin journal, which I have now come to love, to write lists in. Please note that my new name is Precious Golden Lily. I live in the summer wing of the Peacock Pavilion, and I am lady-in-waiting to Empress Magnolia, who is not quite beautiful and extremely ill-tempered.

what i did in my holidays
    got bored
    cut my fringe (it went a bit wonky)
    tidied my room
    talked to Jakob
    rented 4 videos for 4 dollars: *101 Dalmatians,*
        Practical Magic, Shrek, The Matrix
    helped Mum weed the garden
    began making lists
    made a carrot cake with cream cheese frosting
    wondered if I should get a mobile phone
    decided not to get a mobile phone

things you either

went swimming by myself at the river
began talking to myself
did not get a job at Video World
lost a kilo
put it back on again
found myself a job!!!

Funny how things turn out. On January 4th I got a letter from Video World, saying thanks but no thanks. It was not a surprise. The envelope also contained a free Latest Release Video Voucher, which was. Stuart had written 'Good Luck with your job hunting, Georgia', in red pen at the bottom of the typed letter. Nice one. Maybe in another life we'll fall in lerve and get married. I can visualise it now. Two chubby couch potatoes wearing matching tracksuits, bonded by our fondness for films and our passion for pizza. On second thoughts, this is not a good idea, not even in a future life.

Anyhow, back to the subject of me and my brilliant career.

(Jakob, I will get to your concert yet.)

On January 5th I was bored out of my skull. You'd need to be to read the local freebie paper from back to front, but that's how I spent my morning. There was an inspiring article about a ninety-six year old grandmother who gets around in her blue Volkswagen Beetle. She visited the Great Wall of China when she was a mere gal of eighty. Go girl! I can tell you the price of gourmet potatoes at Victor's Vegie Mart, and the venue for 'Yoga with Sudhassana' on Monday nights. I whiled away a good hour, multi-tasking as I read. I managed several small but important jobs such as filing my nails, drinking two mugs of coffee and rearranging my hair. The last section of the paper was particularly thrilling. The personal column. Garage sales. Lost and found. Work wanted. Situations vacant. And there it was. The very thing.

> *Wanted. Part-time bakery assistant.*
> *No experience necessary as full training will be given.*
> *Suitable for high school student.*
> *Mainly holiday and weekend work. Immediate start.*

Me, Me, Me, I shouted, leaping to my feet and zooming into action. All right, I didn't actually shout it out loud but I thought it at top volume. Applying for a job the second time around was easier than the first. I already had the outfit and the portfolio, all I needed was a large dose of courage. Remembering Mum's pep talk, I said an affirmation or two as I brushed my hair and fumbled with the clasp on the crystal necklace.

I am a winner.

Heavenly Delight, I am the very angel you need.

❀

I walked to the shopping centre as I didn't want to arrive sweaty, with flattened hair, like last time. If Mum had been home she'd have driven me but work can't spare her right now, so I have to do my own thing these holidays. I don't mind walking, anyhow. I like looking at gardens, especially when people have made efforts, like the Italian man whose concrete yard is decorated with planters made from car tyres. They're shaped like swans and are painted orange and turquoise. Snazzy. Sometimes I talk to cats. Cats are witchy. They answer me with their eyes.

things you either

While I walk I play a game I invented, called *Perhaps*. As people approach I try to guess whether they'll say hello. The less likely they look, the bigger smile and greeting I give them. Most people respond, one way or another. Some with a genuine greeting, some with a shy mumble. Only occasionally does anyone ignore me. Today playing *Perhaps* amuses me and helps take my mind off my nerves about the job interview. I encounter two mumblers, a smiler, and a middle-aged man who surprises me by saying 'Hello, gorgeous.' When I arrive at the mall I feel a lurch in my guts, but there's no turning back.

I don't like malls. I prefer quirky shops, real shops with real people in them. Malls are Could-Be-Anywhere places. They lack soul. All those boring chain stores with fake air, fake music, fake people. When I grow up I'm going to write a PhD on the cultural destruction caused by malls, but now is not the time so don't get me started. At least the bakery is on the outside of the shopping complex, not in the dead plastic heart.

⁌♡⁍

Well, here I am. I don't want to lose what little courage I have, so I go straight in. A dark-haired woman about the same age as my mum is serving a spunky looking guy. She selects the two pesto scrolls nearest her with a pair of silvery tongs, tucks them neatly in a brown paper bag, deftly twists the top.

'That'll be five dollars, thanks.' The spunky guy, a Logan clone with curly hair and a basketball under his arm, has the money ready. He bites into the first scroll before he's even left the shop.

'Can I help you?'

'I've come about the job. The part-time one that was advertised in the *Leader*.'

'Good. I'm Jude, I'm the manager. What's your name, and how old are you, luvvie?'

'I'm Georgia, and I'm fifteen.'

'Have you worked in a shop before, Georgia?'

'No, but I'm a quick learner and I'm very reliable. I've got my Personal Portfolio here if you'd like to have a look.'

'Great. How about you leave it here for me to have a squiz at when I get a chance. Can you start tomorrow morning?'

'Yeah, sure.'

'Terrific. Come back at four when things quiet down and I'll give you a bit of training. We can sort out your uniform and you can fill out a tax form.'

'Four o'clock. Okay, I'll be here.'

'Righty ho, see you later then.'

❤

Whoop-de-do and pass the peanut butter. It looks like I just got me a job.

I'm so dazed and confused that I wander into the mall by mistake. The first sight I see is Eva, checking out the sale bin outside the shoe shop. She looks great, as always, in apricot shorts and an orange halter top, but there's a big bandage on her knee. Too late, she's waving. Oh no. I have to go over, I guess.

'Hey, Georgia. What's up?'

'Not a lot.' There's an awkward silence.

'Hey Georgia?'

'Yeah?'

'I'm sorry I was rude to you at the party. The vodka kind of messed with my head.'

things you either

'No worries. Thanks for saying sorry. I shouldn't have nicked your drink.' I'm still feeling embarrassed but I'm pleased she apologised.

'Guess what?' I continue. 'Something good just happened. I got a job in the bakery.'

'A holiday job?'

'Yeah, and after school and weekends too, I think. Not sure of the details yet but I start tomorrow.'

'Nice one. Did you hear what happened at the party after you left?'

'What?'

'Logan dumped Poppy. He's seeing a girl who goes to St Hilda's. Poppy is totally gutted.'

'I can imagine.'

'And guess what else? Finn and Hannah aren't an item either because Finn got so tanked that he passed out on the lawn, right where I chundered, actually. It was disgusting. Hannah threw a hissy fit and went home by herself. Reckons she's tired of dealing with a stoner.'

'Yeah, well, he was pretty out of it.'

'It didn't worry Emma, though. You should have seen her make a play for Finn. She was, like, all over him. Once he woke up, of course.'

'What happened to your leg?' I ask, floundering for something to say. I'm appalled and delighted by her account of Saturday night's events. The great soap opera of life, broadcasting right now at your local mall.

'Got stabbed by my tiara. It was hidden in the bean bag and when I sat down it cut my thigh open. It's gone septic.'

'Bummer.'

'What are you doing now, then?'

'Going home. I've got some stuff to do before I come back for my training.'

'Well, see ya then. Hope the job goes great and everything.'

'Cheers. Good luck with your leg.'

I walk home, or rather I float. I am happy happy happy. The day is bright with miracles. I am now employed and Eva, the scary person, was nice to me. Tra la la. Peonies and dog shit. The world at my feet.

❦

I ring Mum at work. When I tell her my news she's seriously stoked. I put on Jack Johnson and dance around to my favourite track. I make a ham and lettuce sandwich with only a smidge of butter, pour myself a pineapple juice. It's the sort of lunch a thin person would eat. Perhaps I'm transforming into a new and better version of myself: elegant, confident and, best of all, rich as hell. I start to phone Mel with the party gossip and my big news but then I remember she's away, so I tell Jakob all about it instead. He's rapt. Then I blob and watch Oprah until it's time to leave. I enjoy Oprah. Her shows cover some meaningful topics, plus she's honest about her weight problems. She'll never be thin. Her eyes light up with glee whenever she mentions fried chicken or chocolate brownies.

🕶

I go to the bakery at four and by the time I get home I'm shattered. My brain is crammed so full that I wouldn't be surprised if some of the things I'm supposed to remember come squeezing out my ears. I'm supposed to know the names of all the products and what they look like, but there

things you either

are so many different breads and other items that I'm bound to forget some, especially if I'm nervous, which I am. I've got a tax form to fill in, and a diagram of the till to study. There's a different till code for every item. Sounds easy, but there's heaps of ways you can get it wrong. If the till doesn't balance at the end of the day you have to explain why, and replace the missing money if there's a discrepancy. Man, I hope I don't stuff that part up. I'm going there to *make* money, not to lose it.

The worst thing of all is the uniform, pale blue with a white collar. I look totally shite in it. I bulge in all the wrong places. My blue cap is seriously silly, and I have to pull my hair back in a ponytail or wear hairclips. Most unflattering. I try the whole lot on to show Mum. She pretends I look fine, but I don't. I resemble Mrs Gladys Goofy, a matronly woman who was born on a chicken farm and should have stayed there. I feel stressed out but Mum has got Indian takeaway and a bottle of sparkling grape juice to celebrate, so I get a grip, for her sake.

❦

Dinner is delicious. I forget about being the new slim elegant Georgia and eat plenty of butter chicken, scooping up the sauce with my garlic naan bread. After tea I go to my room to study my diagram of the till. I'm fully engrossed in sourdough ciabatta ($4.95, Code 7) and granary sliced ($2.95, Code 11) when I hear Mum yell 'pick up the phone'. It's Mel. Usually her calls are a pleasure but not this time. She's over the moon with joy because not only has Toby phoned her twice but now he's hitching down to see her.

'I think we might be, you know... going together,' she confides. 'And guess what else, Georgie? My skin has improved a lot since we got here. My dad reckons it must be the sunshine and salt water.'

'That's fantastic, Mello.'

'Are you okay? You sound kind of funny.'

'Nah, I'm okay. I'm happy for you, really I am. I'm just a bit spooked about tomorrow.'

'You'll be fine, girl. You'll be great. You'll be Georgia, queen of the bakehouse.'

'Yeah, maybe. The money will be good, for sure. $8.70 an hour, more on the weekend. Concert here I come! Just wish I didn't look so awful in the outfit.'

'You're gorgeous and don't you forget it. Will you always be working on the weekends, then?'

'Only some. The roster changes each week, Jude says.'

'I hope you get some weekends off, so we can hang out together. I wish you were here, it's great. I've been swimming heaps. Haven't found you a seahorse yet, but I've got you two starfish, a marble with whirly bits and some tiny purple shells.'

'Beautiful. So how long is Toby staying?'

'Till Wednesday. He only gets two days off from his Video World job. Mum's going to make him sleep in the bunkhouse.'

'Well, have fun, Mello. See you when you get back, hey.'

'Love you, Georgie. Love you in stars and roses.'

'Love you in diamonds. Okay, bye.'

❀

When Mum comes to say goodnight I'm lying face down on my bed having a big loud cry.

'What's the matter, sweetie?' Her voice is a mix of love and worry.

things you either

'Everything. Now that I've got a job it feels really scary and Mel's going out with Toby so she won't need me any more. Everything's changing, and I'm tired of being fat. I look like a goddamn armchair in my uniform.'

'Oh, Georgie.' She hugs me and I tuck into her shoulder, enjoying her familiar sweet and musky scent.

'You'll be fine at the bakery. Truly you will. Everyone gets nervous when they start something new. As for Mel, be happy for her, Georgie. She deserves a bit of romance in her life. Lastly, you're not fat, you're curvy. You look lovely.'

'Bunkum,' I mumble, wiping my nose. I want to believe her. I do. But the hard lonely place inside me feels so vast and empty that her tenderness just slides down and vanishes.

After Mum turns off the light I lie awake. I can't even bear to talk to Jakob. I toss and turn in the dark shadows until I drift into sleep.

banking on it

Well, it's official. I've survived my first day at work. At first I was out the back doing menial stuff like sweeping and learning how to work the bread slicer. After the lunch rush, Jude put me on the counter, and I handled it okay. I only made one minor mistake when I gave a man the wrong loaf of bread. Sun-dried tomato ciabatta looks exactly like olive ciabatta to me. They're both dotted with indistinguishable dark bits that could be dead flies. Luckily the customer spotted the difference and came back to exchange loaves.

There's a guy called Lee who works at the bakery. He's nineteen and studying engineering at uni. He told me all about himself in great detail. Lives in a flat with two other guys, plays hockey competitively, trains three nights a week, blah blah blah. He neglected to tell me that he's Jude's nephew. That only came out later when she mentioned it. Earlier in the day I'd said 'Jude seems really nice', and Lee just grunted. Good thing I didn't say she was a nasty cow.

I suppose he's not bad looking. Tall, medium build, with short brown hair, and an emerald stud in one ear. But something about him makes me uneasy. He's such a know-it-all, for one thing. He tells me what to do and how to do it far more than is necessary. When Jude went to do her grocery shopping he completely freaked me out by pretending to chop his fingers off with the bread slicer. I told Mum about it and she reckoned he was trying to impress me, but there are better ways. How about two tickets to see Natural Affinity or a smooth remark about my superior intelligence and wonderful smile? You have much to learn, dodgy boy.

Anyway, my first day at work is over. We're allowed to take home one free item, and the rest goes to a women's refuge, which is kind of cool. I chose a wholemeal sesame cob, and we're having it for tea with Greek salad. Yummoh.

My Favourite Bakery 🍞 Products
Sweet Chilli Twist
Almond and Custard Log
Apricot Pecan Loaf
Herb and Garlic Twisty
Sun-dried Tomato and Olive Focaccia
Apple and Walnut Rolls
Danish Berry Lattice
Apricot Scrolls
Fruit Buns
Chocolate Croissants

things you either

Silly things this world could do without
 BLONDE jokes
 Stickers on FRUIT
 WEBSITES for things such as origami boulders
 SEXIST jokes
 TOO MANY piercings
 BRAZILIAN WAXING
 Chihuahuas
 RASCIST jokes
 THOSE who spend all their time TXTing
 Cigarettes
 The use of the word ISSUES if not meaning library books
 MALLS
 Soap shaped like chocolate
 Chocolate shaped like soap

Things i want to do before i die
 Travel the world
 Live in Thailand
 Learn to sing
 Find a black kimono embroidered with gold dragons
 Get a rabbit
 Love someone fully
 Talk to the real Jakob instead of the paper Jakob
 Have twins (maybe)

I'm writing lots of lists at the moment because, apart from work, my life consists of little. Mum goes to work and comes home tired. Mel is staying at the beach until school starts. It wasn't the original plan but her parents have found someone to look after their gallery so now they're staying the entire holidays. I could have gone down if it wasn't for the bakery. Anyhow, this week I did three and a half days. I've earned the grand sum of $168, minus tax, which won't be much, I hope. Mum says I don't have to pay her back the ten bucks. Cool.

IN		OUT	
Bank	$40.00	$15.00	Dress hire
Gilda	$10.00	$3.00	Chocolate (large bar)
Babysitting	$30.00		
Bakery	$150.00 after tax?		

BALANCE = $212.00

Thus I am moving steadily towards my goal. At this rate I should well be able to afford to go. Originally Mel and I were going together, but now she and Toby are hanging out, perhaps she won't want to go with me. That part I don't know about yet but I tell you, Jakob, I'll be there, no matter what.

two weeks later

The weather is hot hot hot. Mum's been grumpy as hell lately. She has some difficult stuff happening at work, like a big new computer system that keeps crashing, and she's worried about Kevin and Joy. They're seeing a marriage counsellor, and Gilda has gone to stay with Sooze for awhile. When I heard about the counsellor I knew things were serious. Mum said Gilda could stay with us but Sooze was keen to have her. Even sent some money towards the airfare, which borders on the miraculous. So Gilda's gone north to Sooze's. I'm left here with my mother who is unhappy and who asks me too many questions. She constantly pokes

things you either

her nose into my life. She comes into my room looking miserable and asks boring shit. I hate it.

I miss Mel heaps. As for work, it's okay. I've got the till and the products well and truly sussed now. Jude is great and I like Kate, the other girl who works there part-time. We both work Saturdays, the busiest day. Kate is seventeen, a surfie girl with bleached hair and a fine sense of humour. We make up names for the regular customers, some of whom are very weird. Mrs Date Scone, for example. Comes in most afternoons around three o'clock, spends ages looking at everything and usually leaves without buying anything. Very occasionally she asks for 'one date scone, please'. Then there's Mr Stinky. He has purple veins on his nose, and a strong smell about him. Even in hot weather he wears a thick coat. Jude says to give him two items but only charge for one, so when he asks for a pie we give him two. He never acknowledges it but I guess he appreciates it. This world is full of lost and lonely people, that's for sure.

The guy who looks like Logan comes in nearly every day. He must live nearby. Never buys anything sweet. If we've run out of pesto scrolls, he goes for the cheddar twists. Doesn't take any notice of me, though. I think he's got a thing for Kate, and who can blame him? One pretty surfie chick, gift-wrapped to go. When I tease her about it she says 'No way, Georgia', but then she blushes slightly, so I reckon she fancies him too.

Even though he doesn't know I exist, there's something about this tall striking boy that appeals to me. It's a quality, an energy field. He knows how to hang loose, or he's happy in his body or something. He's also got the most gorgeous smile. A real smile. He's out of my league but hey, there's no harm in admiring him. His name is Hunter. I found out one day when he came in with his friend. They'd been skating and they'd worked up an appetite. Completely cleaned us out of pesto scrolls.

Lee, however, really annoys me. I hate his stupid sexist jokes and the way he acts as if he owns the place. Whatever I do is wrong, according to him. For example, the other day I was sweeping crumbs from the shelves into the dustpan so the floor wouldn't get dirty and he insisted I sweep them straight onto the floor. He has to be right about everything. He's always perving on me, staring at my body instead of my face, and his personal habits suck, big-time. I saw him picking his nose and wiping it on his shorts when he thought no one was looking, which was a total gross out, plus he scratches his nuts all the time.

I wish I could ignore Lee but he shits me with his staring and his babe jokes. I'm sick of being contradicted and sneered at. The guy lacks respect. Last Tuesday I couldn't find my cap. As I was running late, I fronted up without it. Jude was nice, just said I couldn't serve customers due to health regulations. But Lee then made a point of mentioning how short we were of counter staff about a thousand times. I tell you, he's is a genuine A-hole! (The mad thing was that as soon as I got home I found my cap in my wastepaper basket. I have no idea how it got there.)

Mum says ignore Lee. Mum says rise above him gracefully. Mum says if I let him get to me, then he wins. Mum says life is full of annoyances and the trick is to just be happy anyway.

How come I want to stab Lee with a bread knife?
How come Mum doesn't seem happy, anyway?

things you either

Jobs I DO NOT wish for

Dentist (who wants to look up people's noses?)
Bike Courier wearing disgusting lycra outfit
Filleter in a fish factory
Telephone sales of any sort
Mortician
Michael Jackson's surgeon
Michael Jackson's lawyer
Head of the complaints call centre at the tax dept
Policewoman in a hell-rough suburb
Fat girl for singing telegram company

especially good words

vanilla
dodgy
stardust
moonstone
abracadabra
pod
snowflake

Jobs I WOULD like

Roadie for Natural Affinity
Owner of a restaurant in New Mexico
Producer of hip-hop records in LA
Hairdresser for a groovy millionaire
Diving Instructor in The Bahamas
Peony grower
Travel Writer for the *New York Times*
Free-thinking Cuban poet
Famous actor with tattoo of starfish on my shoulder

hate or love   71

Mum says I should go to visit Grandpa Joseph. She is really shitting me at the moment. She keeps barging into my room, picking things up off the floor and putting them in the wrong place. It's very invasive. Anyhow I said I would go. He's the only grandparent I have. Well, that's not actually true, but he's the only one I care about.

My father's parents, the Reeves, live on the Gold Coast. We don't see them any more. When I was eleven they flew me up for a visit. It was the worst week of my life. Everything in their apartment was a soft shade of peach or cream, chosen from some expensive store, everything matching everything else. The only cool things were the photo albums. Sometimes Grandmother Reeves relaxed enough to sit with me, sharing stories about my dad when he was growing up, but most of the time she was too busy tidying. Every time I moved she pounced. Each cushion had to be plumped up and neatly positioned at all times. My plate was whisked away, rinsed and put in the dishwasher the minute I finished eating. The sight of a pair of sneakers in the hall brought on an exasperated sigh. It was nerve-wracking. My grandfather tried to rescue me. He took me out for walks on the beach or for an ice-cream, but living with my grandmother seemed to have withered his soul. He was just this sad old rich guy with nothing interesting left inside him. How these two produced a man like my father is hard to understand. He got away from them early, my mother says, and it saved him.

❧

Anyhow, Mum keeps on at me until I visit Grandpa Joseph. He lives by himself in the tiny house he shared with Nana after they sold the family home. It's been two years since

things you either

she died. My grandfather keeps busy in his garden and in his shed, but he's lonely. Mum visits him regularly, but he keeps to himself most of the time. Old age doesn't look like a whole lot of fun to me. Your body gets worn out and hurts more. People you love die and you know that one day, sometime soon, you'll be next. I try not to think about this stuff but sometimes it's hard not to.

When I arrive my grandfather is weeding his potatoes. He's got a folded sack padded under his knees and he gets up very slowly because of his arthritis. 'Me joints need oiling,' he says. But he's glad to see me, as usual.

'Here she is. My favourite grand-daughter.'

'Yeah, yeah. You say the same thing to Gilda. I know you do.' Grandad flashes me a wink, and wipes his hands on his trousers.

'Very good timing, Georgia,' he smiles. 'I was just about to boil the billy.'

We sit together at the wooden table, dipping our gingernut biscuits into strong tea. I tell him about the Matisse book I got with the voucher he gave me. I tell him about the bakery. I even tell him about Lee.

'So he's not the boy of your dreams, then?'

'More like the creature of my nightmares. Mum says not to let him get to me, but he does. I enjoy everything else about the bakery, but Lee is…I dunno, he's just very creepy.'

My grandfather thinks about this for a minute. He takes another biscuit, dips it all the way in, then swallows it in one bite.

'You know what?' he says finally. 'I wouldn't take any shit from this guy.'

'Grandad!' I say, giggling.

'Yes, well. I tried to think of a more delicate way of

putting it, but that expression said it best. Come on, I want to show you something.'

I follow him to the far end of the garden, past the ancient bathtub planted with herbs, the laden lemon tree and the empty clothesline. Beside the compost heap there's a rusty drum. He lifts the lid.

'Yuck! What on earth's that?'

'Cannibal stew.'

'What?' The dark oily brew is floating with weird lumpy bits and it smells foul, exactly like…well, never mind.

'Cannibal Stew. It's the most marvellous fertilizer. I put all my old tea-leaves in there, plus soapy dishwater, garlic, banana skins and plenty of dead insects. Snails, caterpillars, dead flies, anything I can find. Yesterday I got lucky and found a mouse that had been run over. You leave it to brew for a week or two until it's nice and rotten. I got the idea from a gardening book.'

'Brilliant,' I say, moving a bit further away.

'Something else I want to show you.' On a post, almost hidden by a jasmine vine, neatly arranged on a mound of broken blue china, sits an old pair of spectacles, staring out like eyes.

'How do you like my sculpture?' he asks proudly. 'I found those when I was digging a new bed for the carrots. They must have been there for donkey's years.'

'Very creative, my man.' I give him a big squashy hug. I love my grandad so much: his gnarly brown hands, his quiet eyes, his kind heart.

'Another cuppa?'

'Yeah, why not.'

'How's your mother?' he asks, once we're back in the kitchen.

things you either

'I dunno. She's…troubled, I think.' He doesn't look surprised. Raises an eyebrow, waits for me to continue.

'Work's getting her down and she's worried about Joy and Kev.'

'She always was a worrier, your mother. Susan was the wild child. Joy was the gentle soul, and Anna was the one who tried to sort everything out.'

'Yeah, I know, but it makes her miserable. She takes on my stuff, she takes on Joy and Kev's hassles, but she doesn't really get on with her life. She hasn't even been out with a guy since my dad died.'

'Yes, well, I have my own thoughts on that particular topic.' He pours the last of the dark brew into his mug.

'What do you mean?'

'Can't say too much. Wouldn't be right. Never a good idea to put someone on a pedestal though. Feet of clay and all that.'

I don't know what he's on about but I sense it's something important. I want to know more but he's up now, putting the tea things away and glancing at the clock. Nearly six. Time for the news, which he never misses.

'I'd better go. Mum said to ask you if you need anything.'

'No, I'm fine. Bring me something tasty from your shop next time you visit, eh? I've got something for you, though.' He reaches into a drawer, hands me a neatly folded five dollar note.

'Thanks, Grandad, but you don't have to.'

'I know. But if you want to get to that concert, the one by the two strange girls and the funny looking bloke who can't play for peanuts, every little bit helps.'

We both laugh. I played him 'Board', my favourite

Natural Affinity song once. He listened politely, then pretended to tune his hearing aid but he didn't fool me. He was turning the volume way down low. Off, probably.

'They're the best, Grandad.'

'Best my foot!'

'You gave up on music about the time of the Everly Brothers,' I remind him. 'You're missing some fine tunes.'

'Give me Beethoven or Brahms any day.' He strolls to the gate with me, and kisses me goodbye. I give him a smile and cycle away, waving as I go.

❤

Past the faded blue house, the ugly block of flats, the takeaway on the corner. Cut through the alley, onto the main road, dodging the traffic, pedalling as hard as I can. Keeping the smile plastered on my face, like an idiot pretender, until I turn into our street. I feel muddled and messy and low.

Mum is home early, which throws me completely. I was going to go straight up to my room and chill out in peace, but there she is, in the kitchen, unpacking groceries.

'I took a few hours off so I could get the shopping done.' She glances up to greet me, senses my mood.

'What's the matter, hon?'

'Nothing,' I mumble, making my way towards the stairs.

'Well...okay then. Want a cuppa, pet?' Her tenderness makes me feel worse. I'm ashamed, because I can't cope with things, and disloyal, because I'm freaked out by what Grandad said. Another stupid mystery.

'Yeah. I'll be down soon.'

I chuck my sweaty clothes in the laundry basket and turn the shower on, full bore. The water cascades over me, over

things you either

my dirty hair and my podgy body, cleaning off the sweat and the stink and the sorrow. I wash my hair with some new goo that smells of forests, and I stay in the wet until I am wrinkled like a walnut. A walnut that is ready to face the world again.

❦

Mum has made chai, my favourite. Black tea boiled up with milk, ginger, cinnamon and sugar like they drink in India. We sip the steaming sweetness, letting it cool. For once she tactfully avoids asking me what the matter is. I start talking anyway, choosing my topic carefully.

'Being at Grandpa's makes me sad.'

Why, her eyes ask, but they know the answer.

'He's such a sweetie, but his arthritis was bad today. He misses Nana, and one day he'll die and we'll miss him.'

'Yes. All things are impermanent.' Now it's my turn for silence. 'It's a hard truth but facing it has helped me come to terms with my own grief. Do you remember going to stay with Penny when you were five?'

'Yeah. We played cards and she painted my toenails green and we ate strawberries in the bath. It was fun.'

'It was about six months after Michael died. I was falling to bits, and someone suggested I go on a meditation retreat. I spent most of it weeping and the rest of it furious with everyone and everything. All in silence up at the Tibetan centre in the hills. The monk was very smiley but his English wasn't good. He sat at the front on a gilded dais, a squat Buddha surrounded by yellow chrysanthemums, and one of his students translated his teachings on impermanence. I couldn't take much of it in, but what I could absorb, through my rage and my sniffles, was useful.'

'Okay, so everything changes. Everything dies in the end. I get that. But it still hurts.'

'Yes, it does.'

I look at my mother. She's beautiful, even when she's weary. Her face is interesting. Like a map of everywhere. Her hair is a soft waterfall. I know these are odd observations to make in the midst of a conversation about death. However, they cheer me up slightly. Perhaps I'll look like my mother one day. Beautiful and interesting, with admirable hair.

'You can't let death stop you loving. If the knowledge that Grandpa will die some day makes you afraid to love him, then he might as well be dead already.'

'True,' I say. 'But ... '

'What?'

'Nothing.' I want to say, But you're afraid of loving. I want to say that her truths might be true but they feel like a lecture. I would like to ask her about my father, find out what Grandad was hinting at, but I don't know where to begin.

'Have we got any good stuff to eat?' I ask instead.

'Like what?'

'Butter pecan ice-cream. Chocolate mud cake?'

'Afraid not.'

Suddenly she's irritable. The good feeling between us has vanished. I've avoided talking about things and we both know it. Too late now, though. My mother picks up a magazine, flicks through the pages half-heartedly. Maybe she's just tired but I get out of there fast. The last thing I need is a lecture about my comfort eating.

things you either

embarrassing things that have happened to me

Once upon a time I stole a packet of hundreds and thousands when we were at the grocers. I hid them in my undies and the packet broke and the tiny balls went everywhere. When Mum saw my stolen rainbow trail she tried to growl but she couldn't help smiling. She still tells people about it, even though it happened when I was five.

I didn't get invited by Jackie Wilkins and Sandra Chan to be in the Barbie Club. Such things suck when you are only seven. That was when I decided to hate the colour pink.

I was ten years old and already fat. The school nurse said I was overweight, in front of my whole class.

Last term I farted loudly in Science. Everyone knew it was me. At least it was only a loud fart and not a smelly one, though that wasn't much consolation.

Having to wear my blue uniform and dodgy cap.

Getting sacked from the bakery.

This is what happened. Friday. It was hot. Too hot. Sticky scratchy itchy bitchy hot. I'd worked five days in a row and so, unfortunately, had Lee. Jude was having some tiny skin cancers burned off so she left Lee in charge, and man, did he love that. 'Do this, Georgia' and 'Not like that, Georgia', from the time I arrived in the morning until the time I left. Nothing I did was right, according to Mr Dumb F*ck. I was squashing the loaves with the tongs. I wasn't sweeping the shelves properly. My uniform had a smudge on it. Blah blah blah, rhubarb rhubarb rhubarb. Even Kate confirmed that he seemed to have it in for me, when I asked her for a reality check. Half the time the lazy prat just snoozed in his car, leaving me and Kate to run the shop, while the rest of the time he was in full-on control freak mode.

For the first four and a half days I did what Mum suggested. I buttoned my lip and pretended nothing was wrong. I did whatever Lee asked me to, and carried on as best I could.

Five o'clock on Friday, Lee and I were in the shop by ourselves. Kate was only rostered on for the lunch rush and headed off to the beach, the lucky thing, after rolling her eyes like lunatic blue marbles, and wishing me luck. I'd finished sweeping out the back and was taking my coffee break. Hadn't had time for one earlier because the shop was really busy, even after Kate left. Fridays are often hectic, because people buy yummy breads for dinner parties, and croissants for lazy weekend breakfasts. We're allowed one small item to eat with our cuppa and I'd chosen my fave, an apricot scroll. I was sitting on an upturned bucket in our unofficial lunch room, the alley beside the shop, minding my own business, when Lee sticks his head out.

'What are you doing?' he demands in a snotty tone.

'Taking my break,' I mumble with my mouth full.

'You're supposed to check in with me first. We're low on apricot scrolls. You should have chosen something else.'

'I'm so sorry, Lee. Would it be okay with you if I have my tea break now?'

I don't mean to say it so sarcastically. No, let's get real. I absolutely do. He's starting to really piss me off. As we're about to close up and send the remaining stock to the refuge, mentioning the scarcity of apricot scrolls is just him being a total f★ckwit.

'No it wouldn't be okay. I want you to come and start doing the shelves, right now.'

'Okay,' I say, although there wasn't much point, seeing he'd vanished. I skol my coffee and go back inside. I begin packing loaves into plastic containers for the refuge. Lee has his back to me as he counts the money in the till.

'I'll have to tell Jude about your behaviour, you know,' he says importantly, without turning around.

'Pardon?'

'Jude. She needs to know how things have been while she's away. I'm going to have to tell her that your attitude's been really sloppy.'

'Really?'

'Yes, I'm afraid so.'

'Hey, Lee?'

'Yes, what?' He turns around and looks at me with disdain. There's a smudge of flour on the sleeve of his shirt. I aim a french stick at the floury spot. I don't swing very hard, but I do whop him one. Two actually.

'This is from me,' I say. 'And this is from my grandpa.' Then I grab my bag and a loaf of olive ciabatta and I run, almost knocking Mrs Date Scone over in my hurry to get out of the shop.

Here's the hideous bit. Eva and the gorgeous Hunter were outside, looking in the window. I didn't even realise they knew each other. They'd seen what happened and they were clapping loudly and wolf-whistling. Other shoppers gathered round, wondering what was going on, but I just kept on running.

I picked up my bike and cycled to Grandad's house to give him the bread. I didn't tell him what had happened, and I didn't stay long because he was about to eat. His tea was neatly laid out on the table: a salad of greens from the garden with a lonely boiled egg on top, a pear and two biscuits to go with his cuppa.

At the gate we have a farewell hug, and he picks me a sprig of jasmine to tuck in my pocket.

'Love you,' I yell and we both wave madly.

I feel strangely cheerful, almost high, but it doesn't last. I don't go home. I can't face it. I go to Style Junkies instead and moodle around for ages. I love this quiet shop with its treasure trove of quirky crockery, mad ornaments, old postcards and glittery jewels. No one to love or hate, just dusty loveliness and forgotten things. However, I know I'll have to face the music sometime, and I do.

By the time I get home, Jude has rung. Mum is madder than hell. She doesn't bother asking me for my side of the story, just starts blasting me as soon as I walk in the door.

'How could you, Georgia? I mean I know he's been annoying you, but to attack him so viciously.'

'I didn't attack him viciously. I gave him two gentle whacks with a french stick, which bent and went all limp when it bounced off his arm. Lee's exaggerated the whole thing so that I get in the shit and he comes out squeaky clean. Saint F*cking Lee!'

'There's no need for that sort of language, Georgia!'

'Why not? You say it sometimes.'

'Well, I don't say it very often and I shouldn't. Neither should you.'

things you either

'Yeah, right. How come I have to be so frigging perfect and you don't?' I'm yelling now. I can feel rage, hot in my belly. I'd like to lose control completely, to smash something and break it. But one look at the dark mirror of my mother's face and I stop. There is a certain point beyond which we have never ventured, even in our worst moments. Beyond here is dangerous. I take a deep breath and don't speak. I hold the silence carefully, as if it were a broken paper kite. Fragile. In need of repair. I stare hard at the floor and spy tiny rainbow sparkles under the couch. The ordinariness of Christmas glitter lost in the dust somehow helps me feel a bit calmer.

'So, what did Jude say, apart from telling you Lee's version of reality?' I make my voice conciliatory. Fighting with Lee was bad enough; I don't have the energy to fight with my mother as well.

'She said she was very disappointed about what happened and she wants you to ring her at home as soon as possible. Her number's by the phone.'

'Okay.' I grab the piece of paper, head upstairs, turn back. 'Grandpa told me to, you know.'

'He did *not*, Georgia. I actually rang him, because I thought you might be over there, but you'd left. I told him what'd happened, and he mentioned you two had discussed your work situation. Dad said he'd told you not to take any nonsense from Lee but there's no way he'd have encouraged you to attack someone.'

'I didn't attack Lee. I already told you that. I only dinged him, softly.' I stomp up to my room. When I ring Jude she tells me I'm fired. I was expecting that, but she does it more gently than I'd thought she would.

'I realise Lee can be a bit of a pain but he is a family

member so I'm afraid I'm going to have to let you go, Georgia. The way things stand, I don't think having you both working together at the shop is a very good idea.'

'Fair enough.' That suits me just fine. There's no way I want to set eyes on that loser ever again.

'Come in next Tuesday at closing time and I'll fix you up with the last of your wages. I'll make sure Lee isn't about.'

'I don't suppose I could have a reference, could I?'

'I'll have to think about that one.'

'Thanks, Jude. See ya.' As soon as I hang up the phone, there's a tap on the door and Mum comes in, without waiting for me to say she can. She must have been lurking around in the hall, listening, but I don't say anything stroppy because she's carrying a peace offering: orange juice and Tiny Teddies.

'What happened?' she asks quietly.

'I got the sack, natch. But I asked for a reference and Jude said she'd think about it.'

'That was bold of you.'

'Not really. I deserve one. I'm a good worker, and I didn't do anything wrong.' Mum looks doubtful.

'Well, okay, bopping Lee wasn't the smartest thing I've ever done. I'm glad I did, though. He really had it in for me, even Kate said so. He's possessed by the devil, that guy.'

Mum's scratching her ear. It's an odd little mannerism that indicates she's about to broach a difficult subject. Perhaps she summons up a tiny ear goblin who gives her courage to proceed.

'I was wondering whether it would be a good idea for you to see a counsellor.'

'Why, Mum? Because I lost my cool slightly after weeks of provocation? It doesn't mean I'm a looper. Get real.'

things you either

'It's not just what happened today, Georgie. I just think it could be good for you to talk things through with someone, someone who isn't me. I worry about you, you know. For all sorts of reasons. You really let this guy get to you and then there's your comfort eating…' She tails off uncertainly.

'What? Fat girl therapy?'

'Don't take it like that. Life can be tough, and a mother can only do so much. You lost your dad when you were very young… I just think it'd be a good idea for you to have someone else on your team.' My mother is leaning back on my pillows, mournful and exhausted. She looks as if she's about to cry. If she cries, I'll cry. Then we'll both drown.

'I'll think about it, okay?'

'Okay.' Her voice is weary but she sounds relieved. 'Hey, Penny rang earlier. She invited us over later for pizza. What do you think?'

'Sounds like a plan,' I say. 'Let me change out of this goddamn uniform and we can go celebrate the fact that I never have to wear this dumb-arse cap again.'

Ways in which I am DIFFFERENT to my mother

I am fat

I am cynical

I like techno music

I don't like coriander

I don't like pink

I adore Jakob

I am young

I ride a bicycle

I don't have a job

I don't speak Spanish

Ways in which I am LIKE my mother

We both like reggae
We both eat heaps of toast
We have a fondness
for flowers
Our favourite fruit
is the mango
We are strong swimmers
We both love Grandad
Neither of us will
wear orange
We cry in sad movies
We both miss the same man

begininings, endings & leaky chickens

Time is elastic. An hour can drag on forever. A day can last a lifetime, slow as the dripping of a tap. After I got the biff from the bakery the days moved sluggishly. Everything was an effort, like swimming through porridge. I muddled through the hours, filling them with small tasks that amounted to nothing. Mum offered me $5 an hour to do housework, so I did some boring stuff like clean the bathroom and weed the garden. I earned $20 but I was well sick of menial chores.

When I collected my pay, Jude surprised me by handing me a reference. It was only a few lines but said I was a hard worker and a cheerful staff member. I banked my final cheque of $38, but then spent $15 on an impulse buy of a purple silk shirt at The Great Mistake. Actually, when I got home the shirt felt like A Georgia Mistake, but Mum

things you either

swears it looks good. I scoured the paper for another part-time job but I didn't find anything suitable, although being a driver for The Aphrodite Escort Agency sounded like it would have been interesting.

Then all of a sudden, on the last weekend of the holidays, time sped up, moving like a roaring river towards the mighty tempest of Niagara Falls, otherwise known as The Beginning of Term. 'Once more time is slowly passing rather quickly,' I said to Jakob, who is often the only person lucky enough to hear my flashes of brilliance. Mel called me when she got home from the beach. We lay on her back lawn under the pear tree, discussing absolutely everything. Well, let's be honest, we mainly talked about Toby-the-Fantastic, and Lee-the-Utter-Prat. I expected to feel jealous about Toby, but seeing Mel so chuffed I couldn't help but be happy for her. It was me I felt sorry for, because with her skin the clearest it had ever been Mel looked superb. However, as I'd been filling my idle hours eating toasted cheese sandwiches, my black jeans were even tighter than usual, indicating that I had put on extra blobbage. Not good.

·❤·

I hate the first day back at school. The weather goblins always produce a scorching hot day, which, combined with the irritability of the teachers, the chaos of timetables, long queues at the bookshop and the din of a thousand voices catching up on a summer's worth of gossip, adds up to A Very Trying Experience. I came home with a throbbing headache, clutching a timetable that wasn't worth a knob of goat's poo. Mel and I only have one class in common, double Lit on Wednesdays. Worse still, my Friday is the hardest day of the week, when any fool knows it's meant to be the easiest. I whinged to Mum about it, but she wasn't listening. She was busy putting the groceries away and cooking an early tea because she was off to her Amnesty meeting. After dinner she hurried to go, leaving me with a sink full of dirty dishes and strict instructions not to eat the butter pecan ice cream.

'Why the hell not?'

'There's no need to swear at me, Georgia. It's for Friday night. Penny's coming for tea.'

'How come the visitors get all the good stuff?'

'Have an apple if you're hungry,' she snapped, hurriedly applying lipstick as she raced out the door.

'An apple. Oh yes, what a fine idea. I have always found a wizened apple almost as good as a huge slice of carrot cake topped with whipped cream,' I say to no one in particular. Then I check out the freezer to see if we have any other kind of ice cream, but we don't.

If I was a member of Natural Affinity I'd make sure I was surrounded by an abundance of delicious foods. I wouldn't deprive myself of anything, yet I'd remain slender because I'd dance wildly on stage and have mad passionate sex with Jakob the rest of the time. However, I'm not in Natural Affinity and I've never had mad passionate sex with anyone.

Instead, I'm in a grotty kitchen, all alone and feeling sorry for myself, which is quite another story. No boy will ever want to hold the hand of a large girl like me. It's a thin girl's universe and quite frankly, it sucks.

I wash the dishes and leave them to drain, then wander into the garden and throw leaves in the air like confetti. I return to the house and wander aimlessly for a while, exerting a

things you either

huge amount of willpower by not making raisin toast or picking the pimple on my chin. I go upstairs and take out the yellow journal, my trusty friend in times of gloom and sorrow.

10 things you can do with a sausage beside eating it

frame it

talk to it

throw it

sit on it

send it to the prime minister

chop it into small pieces and feed it to the ducks

write a poem about it

bury it at midnight

hide it in your enemy's gumboot

use it to prop up a postcard

stuff I don't like that everyone else likes

reality TV shows

BEER

Strawberry ice cream

ANYTHING strawberry that's NOT an actual strawberry

Lycra

Jelly

Black jelly beans

HIGH HEELS

Red lipstick

MALLS

Dairy Milk chocolate

the colour PINK

THREE MINUTE NOODLES

hate or love   89

I'm wondering whether to write a list of *Ten Scary Technological Things That Might Happen in My Lifetime*, or whether to watch *ER*, when the phone rings, taking me by surprise. Even more surprising is who's phoning me.

'Hi Georgia. It's Eva. Got your number from Poppy, who got it off Mel. I was talking to Toby and he said you were looking for another part-time job. Well, so am I, and guess what? They're looking for check-out operators down at New World, the big one in town, and I'm going there after school tomorrow. You could apply too if you want to. Mrs Jakovich is the woman you have to see. Just thought you might want to know.'

'Hey, thanks a lot, Eva. I am looking for work, seeing I'm no longer at the bakery.'

'Yeah, Hunter and I were kind of blown away by what happened the other day. You were so cool. Hunter used to play soccer with Lee. Says he's a real moron.'

'Yeah. Umm, so…how's your leg?'

'Pretty good actually, healing up quite well. Hunter says the scar looks cute, like a crescent moon.'

'Hunter. He's the guy who came into the bakery a lot, right, but I don't remember seeing him around school. Is he new, then?'

'Nah, he goes to Metro College, the school for ferals and mung-beaners. He's going to try for a job at New World himself. They need heaps of part-timers apparently. Anyhow, gotta go. See ya.'

'Bye, Eva.'

❤

Wow. A phone call from Eva. I may have lost my job at the bakery but I seem to have gained some street cred in the

things you either

process. Hmm. One further thought. It sounds as if Eva and Hunter are an item. I guess Kate will just have to live without him. So will I, but that was always true.

BEING A CHECK-OUT OPERATOR

The No 1 rule is SMILE. If you are not able to smile or be pleasant to our customers this is not the job for you. Use manners AT ALL TIMES when dealing with staff and customers.

UNIFORM: *Keep your uniform clean and tidy. Hair should be tied back from the face. Hands must be spotlessly clean at all times. Wash them if you have dealt with bloody meat or leaky chickens. Clean your conveyor belt and your scanner regularly. BO and ciggie breath are not appreciated by customers.*

NAME TAGS: *To be worn at all times. Replacement fee is $6.00.*

YOUR SUPERVISOR *is there if you require assistance with price checks, enquiries about voids and refunds, credit card signature verification, difficult customers, anything at all.*

STARTING WORK: *Be at work, ready to go onto the checkout, at your start time. Lateness is not acceptable. If you require time off for study you are required to find your own replacement.*

YOUR TILL: *Will be ready for you when you start your shift. Don't open a bag of coins until you have completely run out of that denomination. Place all your notes in the till in the same way, eg, heads up, your end. Your till has 3 numbers to identify it, plus 3 secret numbers to open the register. You are responsible for the money in your till. It must always balance.*

PACKING: *Use large bags for the majority of your packing. Don't over-fill or under-fill. Small bags are for smaller* items or to keep meats, dairy and frozen foods separate. Large brown paper bags are for customers who ask for no plastic. Pack similar items together, eg, cans with cans. Take care with delicate items such as eggs, bread, soft fruit, tomatoes.

PAYMENT METHODS: We accept Visa and MasterCard. No cash out with credit cards.

All righty, all right. I thought being a check-out operator would be a doddle, but, as you can see, it isn't. The full list of instructions went on for three solid pages. It was daunting. I wondered how Hunter, Eva, and the two others who'd fronted up looking for work were faring. One of them was a pale skinny girl, Tammy, who reminded me of Gilda. The other was a kid called Bob whose main claim to fame so far was that he seemed a bit vacant. Were they also suffering information overload? Did they share my dismay about having to handle leaky chickens? Were they secretly sniffing their own armpits to check if their BO level would be the obstacle to their successful career in grocery marketing? Ah well, we'd find out, wouldn't we, when we fronted up for training.

Mum drove me to New World on Saturday. She was off to brunch with some of the Wild Women so she was going my way. Very handy. First Mrs Jakovich played us a training video about customer service. Smile and be polite, even to aggressive idiots and the barking mad. This was obviously Very Important, and by now we all pretty much had a handle on it. Mrs J handed out our uniforms: white shirts

things you either

with a New World logo, and our name badges. The badge was to be worn neatly above the logo. No radical moves like wearing it on the *opposite* side. We could purchase very expensive black trousers at a designated clothing store or wear our own clothing on what Mrs J called 'our bottoms', provided it is NEAT and BLACK and TIDY.

We take turns on the till. First we each fill a trolley with a selection of items then we practise scanning them, with Mrs J hovering around us like a giant talking fly. My initial impression of Bob is confirmed. The guy's a space cadet. He piled his trolley with silly stuff, like condoms, sanitary pads and light bulbs. I could see Mrs J wondering whether to blast him for being ridiculous but wisely deciding to ignore him. Tammy is sweet, but not very confident. Eva, true to form, acts sassy. Knows everything already. Mmm. Hunter must have a different opinion of her, though. I wish I didn't find him so attractive. It's hard to concentrate on sensible stuff when your mind keeps sliding sideways into inappropriate thoughts, such as trying to work out what's tattooed on someone's arm. A Celtic pattern, by the way. Good choice, Hunter.

It's interesting, isn't it, what attracts someone to someone else? I like his looks, true, but it's more than that. He seems like a good person: friendly and helpful and ordinary. He smiles at me several times when Bob acts like an idiot, which is pleasing.

Scanning is an art form in itself, we discover. There's a surprising amount to master, such as smooth wrist motion when sliding the barcode across the magnetic code reader.

'Not like that, Eva. Do it as softly as you can so you don't damage the potato chips.'

We begin to get the hang of it. We learn to scan five

avocados, by scanning the first one and pressing the repeat code. We're shown how to tell different varieties of apples apart. How to do EFTPOS without cash. How to do EFTPOS with cash. Which sorts of cheques are okay. How to do a price look up (plu) on small deli items, such as flowers and bulk dry goods like nuts and lollies. Never say 'Hi.' If someone looks dodgy call a supervisor. DON'T forget to SMILE.

But we never do get to uncover the mysteries of the Christmas Club, because Tammy faints. One minute she's asking what to do about voids, then she collapses gently on the floor, a packet of chocolate biscuits falling from her hand. Mrs J starts fanning her with a piece of the newspaper that's used for wrapping ice cream. El Sleazo, aka Bob, immediately asks if he should loosen her collar, but, luckily for our Tammy, right then she opens her eyes and murmurs, 'What happened?'

'It's all right, dear. You fainted. Do you think you can stand up now? Take it slowly, that's the way.'

Tammy gets up, awkwardly, rising from crumpled to upright, all long legs like a shaky foal.

'Did you eat a proper breakfast before you came in, Tammy?' Mrs J asks. It's a sensible question because Tammy is such a waif she probably had her last proper meal in the winter of 1998.

'Yes I did. I had a muffin and a can of Coke. But I am a wee bit nervous. I do faint sometimes, but not very often.' Tammy's voice is flimsy, her pale cheeks pink with embarrassment.

'Well, all right then, dear. Take it gently and let's just see how you go. That's probably enough for the first day anyway. We don't want you to suffer from information

things you either

overload.' Mrs J pauses and smiles, so we can be impressed by her contemporary choice of phrase. Adults are very obvious sometimes. They lack subtlety. Suddenly I'm ashamed of my cynical thinking. Mrs J was only trying to be nice. Maybe I am screwed up. Perhaps I do need a shrink, not for my weight but because I'm a horrible uncharitable person with a mean-arse attitude.

'Make sure you study your notes carefully before you start work. Here's a copy of your rosters. Any questions?' Mrs J asks.

Bob asks how soon after we start will we get our first pay. Mrs J says not for a fortnight. It will go into our bank accounts every Thursday, and we'll be on the starting rate for 15–17 year olds, which is $8.50 an hour.

I check out the roster. I start tomorrow, Sunday, from 9 am till 5 pm. No sleeping in for me. Welcome to the real world.

🛒

in TWO words

Mrs Jakovich ★ Efficient. Speedy.

Eva ⊚ Sulky. Fragrant.

Bob ★ Dodgy. Gormless.

Hunter ⊚ Interesting. Handsome.

Tammy ★ Dreamy. Shy.

Me ⊚ Dazed. Confused.

Hunter was rostered on all day Sunday, the same as me, but Eva didn't start until the evening shift from five till nine. She wasn't too happy about not being paired up with Hunter, but Mrs J, despite her brisk kindness, has a steely edge. She isn't the sort of person Eva's sultry charm would work on and Eva knew it, so she didn't bother trying to beg, grovel or sulk. Tammy and Bob were rostered on week afternoons for the next fortnight.

On Saturday night I lay awake for ages, anxious about the day ahead. Staying up late, watching the video of *The Ring* all by myself, didn't help the situation. Let me warn you. Do *not* watch that film. You will be scarred for life. You will also be so scared that you will have to sleep with the light on until you are thirty-three years old. But here's the beautiful thing. Sunday was really fun.

I manage to get up, fuel up and leave the house without waking Mum. She's been so cranky lately that I'm glad to get away without her endless questions and reminders. I catch the 8.30 bus to town and arrive at the supermarket in plenty of time. I even remember to give Mrs J my bank details. Hunter races in, puffing, at the very last minute. Mrs J raises her eyebrow but doesn't say anything, just sends him to cut, squash and tie up cartons out the back. Pity. He looks smart in his black jeans and white t-shirt. After giving me the once over for TIDYNESS, Mrs J lets me loose on the general public. At first there aren't many customers so I have time to get the hang of things. When there are no customers I study the product code chart and wipe my screen, scanner and belt.

Having a plastic sign reading 'Trainee Operator' in front of me is a drag. It might as well have said 'Incompetent Fool'. But I didn't make too many stuff-ups. Well, only that incident involving the elderly lady who asked about the Christmas Club. I hit her with a box of cereal until she passed out, then hid her beneath the counter by rolling her under there with my foot. Kidding.

@

things you either

At lunchtime I buy a ham roll from the deli counter, and stroll to the nearby gardens. When I finish eating I feel sleepy. The summery buzzing of flies always has a snoozy effect on me. So does getting up at 7.30 am. I crumble dry lavender heads, take a big fragrant whiff, then curl up and doze off. I'm lost in a dream about a flying wombat with an annoying cough when I wake up to find Hunter standing above me, coughing in a wake-up sort of a way.

'Mind if I join you?'

'Sure.' I sit up and try to organise my hair with my hand, hoping I don't look too dishevelled. 'Is this your first job?' I ask.

'Nah, I had one at Video World, but I got fired.'

'How come?'

'I let a friend have free videos.'

'Oh.' He must have been the guy Toby told me about. The one who got sacked. The one whose job I didn't get.

'Yeah,' Hunter continued. 'It was kind of dumb of me. Honesty is the best policy, don't you think?' I check him out to see if he's being sarcastic, but he seems sincere. He's looking at me like a friendly dog who wants my approval. He's way more gorgeous than Logan. They both have curly blond hair and they're both tall and skinny, but Hunter has a more open expression, unlike Logan, who looks like someone who adores himself.

Hunter also has the most amazing green eyes. I'm staring at him. I offer up my own lost job story.

'Yeah, I got sacked too, as you no doubt heard, because of what happened the afternoon you and Eva saw me at the bakery. They don't like the workers to use the bread as weapons, strange as it may seem.'

'It was hilarious though, what you did to Lee. He's such a loser.'

'Maybe so,' I mumble. 'But my mother didn't find it amusing. She thinks it proves I'm bonkers. She wants me to see a counsellor.' Shit. Why on earth did I blurt that out? Once Eva finds out it'll be all round the school.

'So, what are you going to do with the fortune you're about to make in the grocery industry?' Hunter asks. I tell him my plan about the Natural Affinity concert.

'Fine band. I love that track 'Flip', superb guitar solo.'

'What about you? Any plans to buy a fast car or a ticket to New York?'

'I'm thinking of getting a dog, to hang out with when my life feels like crap. I go through a fair few skate decks, too. I've made a coffee table out of my broken ones.'

'Really. That must look cool. Hey, what time is it?'

'Time we got back. Goodbye flowers. Goodbye trees.'

Another thing I like about this guy is his nutty sense of humour. I want to ask him things, like why his life feels crap, and what sort of dog he wants, but I'm too shy. We wander back in silence. It feels like an awkward silence to me but who knows, it might be a comfortable one as far as Hunter is concerned.

❤

The minute we get inside the door Mrs J appears, scowling.

'It's ten past! Make sure you get back on time in future please. I've put Lucy and Dan on the tills until five. You two can do some unpacking. Come with me.' She takes Hunter to Aisle 7 (Pasta, Rice, Sauces) and me to Aisle 2 (Biscuits, Crackers, Spreads). I spend several happy hours unpacking cartons of biscuits and savouring my favourite flavours in the kilojoule-free zone of my imagination.

When it's nearly time for our shift to end, Mrs J sends me to fetch a mop so I can clean up the sticky area where some airhead dropped a bottle of sweet chilli sauce. I pretend it's dinosaur blood and clean it up, no worries. On my way back I notice a woman with variegated orange hair talking animatedly to Hunter, who's stacking tins of pasta sauce. They can't see me but something about this wacky woman intrigues me, so I lurk about, fiddling with packets of dried fruit on a nearby shelf.

'Now, I know this isn't your fault, sunshine, but I want you to pass my complaint to the appropriate person. Tell them an outraged customer finds it an insult to her intelligence.'

'Um, what exactly is the problem?' asks Hunter, puzzled.

'Look at this!' She gestures to the SPECIAL notice above the pyramids of pasta sauce. 'It says this is on special for $2.99. But the usual price is $3.00, therefore it's going to scan at exactly the same price it always did. It's ridiculous.'

Hunter thinks for a second, then looks her straight in the eye.

'Lady,' he says cheerfully. 'I couldn't agree with you more. The universe is absurd. Particularly this corner of it. Abandon your intelligence at the door, that's my advice to you.' He gives her a charming grin and the woman wanders off, bemused, down Aisle 8 (Cleaning Products, Tissues, Toilet Paper). I watch her go, admiring her marmalade hair. Hunter sees me watching and beckons me over. I giggle and he joins in until we're both laughing hysterically. When one stops the other starts again. It's pure joy.

Suddenly it's time to go home. Eva arrives for her shift, looking stunning. She smells like gardenias and clouds. I've gone back to not liking her, for obvious reasons, but she's still in friendly mode towards me.

'So,' she says, in the ladies cloakroom, taking off her yellow sun-frock and pulling on a white tank top and a black mini-skirt, which show off her muscular legs and perky boobs to perfection. 'I heard Mel and Toby are an item, hey? Pretty cool, hey?'

'Yep.' I smile feebly. Being with Eva is no fun for me. I glimpse myself in the scratched mirror, as bulgy and plain as ever.

As I leave the building I glance casually around but Hunter's nowhere to be seen. Bob and Tammy are sitting together on a bench, eating McDonald's, which is weird because they aren't working today. It appears that greasy Bob has made a move and that Tammy is too timid or daft to duck for cover. His arm is strategically draped over her skinny shoulders and he's wearing a t-shirt with Metallica on it. A crime against good sense and good taste Bob, my man. They've spotted me. Tammy is waving, so I go over and hang out for a bit.

'Mrs J seems quite nice,' says Tammy. I agree. Bob grunts.

'Scanning's okay once you get the hang of it,' says Tammy. I agree. Bob grunts.

'I'm full. Anyone want to finish this?' Tammy asks. Bob grunts.

'Yeah, I will,' I say. There's nothing like a chocolate thickshake on a hot day. Too rich, too sweet, too cold, too thick. Fabulous.

Tammy's sister picks her up in a battered green Mini and Bob wanders off towards the city, with a final farewell grunt. I wait ages for my bus. When it finally comes I'm the only person on it, which makes me feel even more of a lonesome cowgirl. When I get home I raid the fridge. I eat an apricot yoghurt, six crackers with cheese and a piece of spinach pie. Now I feel sick, as well as lonely.

In my room I take out my calculator and check my money situation. If I earn $90 every weekend for the next month and I don't spend any money, I should have what I need to go to the concert. This should be a triumphant realisation but I still feel flat, tired and shitty. I feel like writing some lists. Lists are good. Lists are safe. Lists contain absolutely no kilojoules. In the land of lists I am not Doofus Girl. I am Georgia, Philosopher Queen. Loved by all and desired by every gorgeous boy in the land. On second thoughts, one gorgeous boy would be plenty, as long as I get to choose which one.

Things I Want
    A magic bicycle
    Two tickets to NATURAL AFFINITY
    A Vietnamese blue silk eiderdown
    To see a ghost
    Eva to shift to another planet
    A cyborg to clean my room
    Purple tulips
    Hunter's generous smile

When Mum comes home she asks me how I am. I say fine, which is a lie.

'Work was okay,' I mumble, glaring at her when she asks for details. I wish she'd leave me alone and stop asking me questions. When I won't talk to her she gets poopy, but

I'm past caring. She needs to get on with her own life and stop sticking her nose into mine. I'm tired of her little lectures and her solicitous enquiries. I turn on the telly and watch *Judge Judy* with my brain switched off.

I pick at my dinner. I'm not hungry but can't admit it. Mum takes it as an insult when she cooks a meal and I won't eat it. I manage the omelette and chuck away the salad when she goes to answer the phone. It's a tele-marketing person. Mum always fobs them off, but gently, because she feels sorry for the poor uni students who take the job.

She makes a cup of tea and starts rabbiting on about Joy and Kevin's marriage therapy. Apparently they're learning about Active Listening and I-messages. At first I think Mum is saying Eye Messages, but no, I-messages are about owning your feelings. For example, it's better to say 'I'm feeling hurt,' than 'You've wrecked my life, moron!' That would be a You-message. These are not recommended.

Active Listening is equally fascinating. When someone whinges, you listen with your heart, letting them know you've heard what they're saying. 'You sound really upset,' is a better reply than 'I've had a gutful of your toxic outpourings.' It doesn't take a very large brain to realise that if Joy and Kev employed these sensible tips their marriage would improve. Who knows, they might even be elevated to sainthood. Saint Kevin, patron saint of Superb Listeners and Saint Joy, patron saint of Owned Feelings.

'Thrilling stuff,' I say. Mum looks hurt. I should feel sorry for her but it's me I feel sorry for, because I am trapped in a boring house with a tedious mother. I stomp upstairs, heavy with irritation. There he is. Jakob. No need for a special appointment. My very own shrink. Pity about his totally useless methods. All he ever gives me is that stupid

things you either

vacant look. I feel anger rising in me, a strong energy pulsing in my chest, my belly, my legs.

So, Jakob. How come Mel doesn't tell me stuff any more? How come the first boy I ever fancied prefers Eva to me? She's just a pretty girl with a cruel streak and skinny legs. Her scar doesn't look like a crescent moon to me. It looks like a wrinkly little scar. How come some people are born beautiful and some are born chunky? And, while we're at it, how come I have two mad aunties, a sad mother and no goddamn father at all?

I'm furious now but Jakob just stares at me with blank eyes. You're an idiot, I hiss at him, so Mum won't come running up to see what's happening. You're only made of paper and I'm sick of you. Even Fifi and Hayley don't like you any more. They're gonna flick you off, gonna start their own girl band called Juicy Flowers, and you're gonna end up playing covers all by yourself in a shitty little pub, full of old men drinking beer and talking bullshit, with no one even listening to you.

I pick up my favourite candle holder and throw it at him as hard as I can. It shatters and tiny shards of blue glass fall all over my bed.

Then I slump on the floor, overwhelmed with sadness, until I can be bothered getting up. I wrap a scarf around my hand so as not to cut myself, scoop the broken glass into the bin. Then I put my *Do Not Disturb* sign on the door, take half the sleeping pill I stole last time Aunty Sooze visited, and I sleep for a thousand years with no dreams.

just another day

I meet Mel at lunchtime under our tree. I'm in a bad mood with everything and everyone and that's that. I sit in

hate or love   103

grumpy silence, munching my way through my fruit-and-nut mix without offering her any.

'Whassup?'

'You really want to know?'

'I just asked, didn't I?'

'All right then. You're supposed to be my bestie, Mel. We used to tell each other everything. So what's this Toby secret you can't tell me? You said he has problems but you won't tell me what they are.'

Mel just sits there, cross-legged like a girl Buddha. Very still and peaceful. Except she's sitting on a dry brown patch of grass instead of a white lotus blossom. Also I can see her black undies a bit, although I try not to look. 'It's not mine to tell.'

'What?'

'Toby's stuff belongs to Toby.'

'Yeah right. Whatever.' The fruit-and-nut mix is crap. Two almonds, heaps of stale peanuts, a few wizened sultanas and an ancient slice of dried banana.

'The thing is, Georgia, I just find it annoying that you think you're the only one who agonises over the way you look. You're not, you know.'

'I don't agonise.'

'Yeah, whatever.' She gives me one of her droll looks. I grin.

'All right, so what's Toby got to worry about, then?'

'I don't feel that great about talking about him behind his back, so this is between us, okay? Firstly, he thinks he's too skinny. He's scared of sport. He hates it but pretends to like it so he'll fit in and be one of the crew. Take skating. He can't get the hang of it. All his friends are going for it, but he can't even master the basic moves. Going camping

things you either

freaks him out because he has a deformed toe. He doesn't want anyone to see him with his shoes off.'

'Oh. A deformed toe. Poor Toby.' I stifle a giggle. Don't want Mel to get huffy.

'There's something else,' Mel adds tentatively. She looks pale, and I notice a few blemishes, though her skin is heaps better these days.

'Oh?'

'You have to promise you won't tell anyone, Georgia. I mean it.'

'I promise.'

'His father just shifted out to live with his boyfriend.'

'Whaat?'

'I know. It's pretty full-on stuff. His mother spends half her time raving about lawyers and revenge, next minute she's crying and begging him to come home.'

'Not good. How did she find out he's gay?'

'Mark, the boyfriend, rang up and outed him. Got sick of being the backstreet boy, as he called it. Toby's mother went psycho and started throwing things into the swimming pool. Chucked his mobile in, and his best silk shirt. Toby and his father had to physically restrain her when she got her hands on his laptop. Once she quietened down she turned nasty, made him pack his clothes and leave, right there and then.'

'Jeez. Poor Toby.'

'Poor everyone.'

I'm stunned. I search for something easier to deal with. 'Jeez. How was your weekend?'

'Okay. Except that on Saturday we went to the beach and I did something I feel weird about.'

'Yeah?' I aim for an accepting tone. I know what's

coming. She's going to tell me they had sex. I'm embarrassed but I don't want Mel to know. If I'm going to be left behind as my best friend ventures into the world of love and lust, at least I can appear gracious.'

'Promise you won't hate me?'

'Don't be daft, Mello. You'd have to do something really dreadful for me to hate you. So, did you murder a little old lady or what?'

'Be sensible or I won't tell you. Okay, here goes. I ate fish.'

'Did you?' I keep my tone non judgmental, and stifle my delight. Whew. So I'm not the only remaining virgin in Golden Bay. However, Mel's face is solemn. I must hold her news carefully.

'I didn't even think it through properly, that's the odd part. I just wanted to, so I did. We walked along the beach for miles, collecting shells. By the time we got back to the bus stop by the takeaway shop I was starving. You could smell yummy fried onions. Toby said he was going to have a cheese burger. He asked if I wanted a salad or juice or something and I just said, 'Nah, I'll have a fish burger.'

'And?'

'It was *delicious*.' Now Mel is giggling, so I can too.

'Your body probably needs the protein or the omega-3 or something. Mum's always going on about how vegetarians have to be careful about nutrition.'

'Could be. I'm having a hard time accepting myself though. I mean, I've been vegan for two years – no honey, no milk, no cheese, no nothing – and then all of a sudden I eat fish.'

'It's not the end of the world, Mel. I mean, if it feels wrong for you, you can always go back to being vegan.'

things you either

She smiles at me, relieved. 'Yeah, you're right, I guess. I need to give the matter some deep thought. So, what's it like being a check-out chick?'

I tell Mel everything about my new career. Well, nearly everything. I recount the absurd universe response and how Hunter and I cracked up over it. I don't mention that I've decided he's a total hottie. I don't want Mel feeling sorry for me because I don't have a snowflake's chance in hell of scoring a drop-dead gorgeous guy, especially one who's going out with Eva.

'Blast, there's the bell. What have you got next?'

'French. You?'

'Media Studies. *Au revoir*, baby. Have fun!'

'Ring you tonight, okay?'

'Kay. See ya.'

❣

I usually enjoy Media Studies. Mr Colgan has a genuine enthusiasm for his subject, but that afternoon seemed to drag on endlessly. Maybe it was because it was a double period and we were doing some dense text analysis. Maybe it was the heat, the afternoon pressing down on me like a sweltering quilt. Or maybe it was because I was tired. I usually get heaps of sleep on the weekends. Working both Saturday and Sunday was catching up on me. Mr Colgan's words droned on like wet bees. My eyelids felt dry and scratchy, my mind wandered out the window, going no-where in particular. I tried to focus but I kept drifting off.

❣

As soon as I got home, I collapsed on my bed. I remember dozing, falling into the welcome arms of sleep. I was dreaming about a dark house with too many rooms, when all of a sudden the phone rang in my dream. It was also ringing outside my dream, in our hall. I answered it groggily, knowing who it would be.

'Hey Mello. Howzit going?'

I heard someone clear their throat, and then a brisk familiar voice.

'Actually Georgia, this is Mrs Jakovich from New World.'

'Hello. Sorry. I was expecting a call from my friend.'

'No problem. Well, not about that, anyway. The reason I'm calling is that I'm horribly short staffed. Bob hasn't arrived and now Tammy can't come in this afternoon. She's phoned in sick, so I was wondering if you were available to do the five to nine shift?'

'Um yeah, I guess so. What time is it now?'

'Let me check. It's 4.20.

'There's a bus every quarter of an hour. I can probably make the 4.45 but I won't get to work till after five.'

'Never mind. We'll pay you for the full shift. It's very helpful of you to come in at short notice, Georgia. I really appreciate it. I won't be here, but Otto, the night manager, will show you what to do.'

❦

I leave Mum a hasty note, grab my uniform and a banana, race to the bus stop. I'm not properly awake and I feel fuzzy as I scrabble for my fare, but by the time I arrive at work I'm nearly normal. As I get off the bus I see Hunter getting out of a beat-up old station wagon, driven by a big guy wearing sunnies.

'Hey, whassup?'

'Hey, Georgia. I'm filling in for Bob. He quit, apparently.'

'He quit? But he never even started.'

'That's Bob, baby. Weird in the beginning, weird in the middle and weird at the end. So what are you doing here?'

'Filling in for Tammy. She's sick. Was that your dad, dropping you off?'

'Nah, my stepfather.'

'Oh,' I mumble. 'What's he like?'

'He's okay. My real father lives in Brisbane.'

'My grandparents live on the Gold Coast.'

'Yeah?'

We stand there awkwardly, not sure where to go next. I want to know more about Hunter, about his world, but now isn't the time or the place.

'Come on then, girl,' he suggests. 'Let's go sell some groceries.'

Otto's pleased to see us. 'Thanks for filling in, kids,' he says, after introducing himself. He's in his forties, and has that shaved head thing that balding guys go for. Otto takes pains to tell us that he's from Austria, not from Germany. He puts me on Check-out 2 and Hunter way down the other end on Check-out 9, which makes it easier to focus on my job. It's busy, with a steady stream of people doing their weekly shopping or picking up last minute items for dinner. You can tell a lot about people by the way they shop.

I'm really tired now. My feet hurt and I'm freaking because I've remembered the Media Studies assignment Mr Colgan dropped on us at the last minute. It's only 750 words but there's no way I'm going to feel like doing anything except crashing when I get home. The music keeps looping around, playing the same three songs over and over again. I'm well sick of *Bridge Over Troubled Water*, *Whiter Shade of Pale* and *Moondance*. I never want to hear any of them again, especially those crappy cover versions. At 7.45 Otto comes to take over from me so I can have my tea break. I sit alone in the staff room, on a hard brown plastic chair at a white table, and eat my banana. I can't be bothered making myself a coffee. The fact that I'm too tired to score myself some caffeine means I'm very tired indeed. I long for the squishy comfort of my bed, but I'd better not shut my eyes or it'll be the end of me. The tragic story of a teenage girl who fell into a deep slumber and spent the night locked in a supermarket with only seventy-nine types of chocolate for company.

⚘

'Otto said to give you a message. Your mum rang, she's going to pick you up.' It's Hunter, here for his break, holding a sports drink and a bag of corn chips.

'Good one. I wasn't really looking forward to going home on the bus. I'm so pooped.'

'Me too. It's tiring coming to work after a school day.'

'For sure. Especially after working the weekend. I'd prefer to just do weekends, if I can swing it.'

'Yeah, me too. Want some chips?'

'Cheers. So what's Metro college like then?'

'I like it. It's pretty laid-back in some ways, but you still have to get your shit together and do the work. It's good not having to wear a uniform. We have a student-centred decision-making process, which makes for some very bizarre discussions. The anarchists don't believe in rules so…'

Just then a ginger-haired girl sticks her head in the door. 'Georgia? Otto wants to know if you got the message from your mother, and he wants you to come back on again now. I'm Leah, by the way.'

things you either

'Hey Leah. I got the message thanks. Okay, gotta go. See ya, Hunter.' He flashes me that scrummy smile again. No boy has a right to be so handsome, but I'm not complaining.

♥

I sleepwalk through the last hour of my shift. The customers thin out, just a few night owls in need of nicotine, and one plump, slow girl with tattooed fingers and wild eyes who buys icing sugar, cream and chocolate sprinkles. I guess there's going to be a late night baking frenzy at her house. I can just see it. 4 am. Now, where did I put those eggs? Hannah wonders, toking on her funny cigarette.

It feels strange being in the supermarket at closing time. I'm in a surreal European movie. Music fades, lights dim. Everyone leaves their aisles in a robotic fashion. Leah, the Polish refugee, tosses back her waterfall of hair as she collects the tills. Except that tonight is the night of an alien invasion...

Back in reality, it's time to go. I can't be bothered getting changed so I grab my backpack and make for the door. Otto works until midnight apparently, supervising the night fillers, but the rest of us are headed home. Otto looks exhausted. The skin around his eyes is whiter than the rest of his face and he moves slowly, as if his limbs are made of heavy metal. I wonder what his life consists of, apart from his job. Maybe he has a sick wife and many children, and he works two jobs to support them. Or perhaps he's a lonely bachelor who goes home to an empty flat and eats cold spaghetti from a tin. This is depressing, so I let my imagination take flight into a fantasy about the empty aisles being taken over at the stroke of midnight by electric-blue tap-dancing budgies.

It's dark on the quiet street. There's Mum, parked outside

and waving to me. Hunter is chatting to Leah as they stroll out the door together. I guess he can't help being such a babe magnet.

my ALL TIME FAVOURITE t-shirt sayings

Beer. So much more than just a breakfast drink
He who dies with the most toys still dies
A friend doesn't let a friend get a mullet
Scary Person
Dopeless and living on hope
Eat More Cherries
51% pleasant. 49% bitch. Don't push me.
Weird is not enough
I am not that bright but I can lift stuff.
RUN!
Sometimes there were a thousand people towards
    a sea of love
Say a Prayer for the Caged
Earth. It's a Twoolygw8place.

Life develops a comfortable rhythm. School, home, work. Work, home, school. Home, school, work. You get the general idea. We never see Tammy or Bob again at New World, which is odd. Mrs J fills the positions with identical twins named Zoe and Lucy, who fall into the Strange category. Lucy has a pierced nose and Zoe has a pierced tongue, which is the only way you can tell them apart. They have matching short butch haircuts and they're into feminism, fantasy literature and lesbianism. The twinnies dress very artistically. They arrive at work in orange plaid mini-skirts, purple crochet tops and black leather army boots, but emerge from the changing room as two ordinary

things you either

check-out girls dressed in black trousers and white shirts, with extremely tidy hair. Amazing.

Hunter works the weekend shift, but we never get the same break, which sucks. There's something about that boy. The way he lopes in, sort of shy but sure of himself as well. I try not to lust after him but am not entirely successful. Inevitably Eva is waiting for him after work, sitting on the bench outside smoking a ciggie, dressed in summery loveliness. At school she's unable to say a single sentence without using the H word. In Lit one day I overhear her talking to Poppy.

'We don't go to his place, because of Jack, his stepfather. He works in a pub at night so he's home in the daytime.

'What's he like?' Poppy asks.

'Hunter finds him a bit difficult. Last time we were there Jack tried to make him take the rubbish out. Hunter refused, because it was mainly Jack's beer bottles. He got shirty so we took off.'

Overhearing this gives me a glimpse into why Hunter described his life as crap. It goes to show that you can't tell what people's situations are like by looking at them. What you see is a guy with a gorgeous smile and a carefree appearance but he has his problems. I've always felt sorry for myself not having a father but at least I don't have to live with a stepfather who isn't that great. I think about Hunter a lot, and catch myself doodling flying hearts around a big curly letter H when I'm supposed to be writing an essay about themes and values in a contemporary novel of my choice. This is not good. I'm turning into a love junkie. I give myself a stern talking to and scrumple the piece of paper up into a tight ball and chuck it in my bin. No point actually courting heartbreak.

Of all the guys I know, how come I've fallen for Hunter? Why not Finn, who's mysterious and dangerous, and a tiny bit like Jakob? Finn who isn't going out with either Hannah or Emma, who mooches around school with oily hair and trodden-on jeans. Why don't I fancy Adrian, the friendly guy in my Media Studies class. I guess that's the X-factor. The magic ingredient. The thing they call chemistry. What a pity this feeling can be overwhelmingly intense for one person and not even present in the object of their affections. I blame it on Cupid, whose arrows make for a cruel world.

That's why it's called a crush, Georgia, I remind myself crossly. Because it crushes you. I hurriedly retrieve the crumpled ball of paper and rip it into tiny fragments in case my mother comes snooping around.

❦

At school everyone is talking about the Year Eleven Camp, to be held at Easter at Hibiscus Bay, a few hours south. Mel and I get out of our classes for the last hour on Friday to help organise the food. We've begun planning the menus; next we'll look at quantities and shopping lists. We want to avoid the awful foods of primary school camps: white sliced bread, cheap sausages, tinned spaghetti. However, with our budget, posh nosh isn't going to be possible. Mel being vegan makes it even harder. We're hunting in recipe books and magazines for suitable dishes. The other people in the team are Adrian, Caris, and Logan. Caris doesn't contribute much, nor does Logan, but Adrian is good value. His parents run a café so he knows a bit about food and has good suggestions, like frittata, and pasta with olives and herbs. He's invited me and Mel to check out the café one weekend but it will be tricky unless I can get time off work.

things you either

Good Names for a Café

The Golden Lotus • RUBY STAR • Kaffeine + Paradiso • Angel Love City • OREGANO • The Silver Dollar • Mermaids • The Holy Belly Button • Peach Blossom • Yum • Passionate Trousers • Naked Lunch

Favourite Comfort Foods

Mashed potatoes
Macaroni cheese
Carrot cake with cream cheese icing

Very Bad Snacks

Stale jam roll with plastic cream, and cold instant coffee
Candle salad: half a banana sitting in a tinned pineapple
    ring with a cherry on top
Fried rat with side dish of dandruff flakes

I'm tired of lists today. I write *The Magnificent World of Georgia, Philosopher Queen, AKA Princess Precious Golden Lily* in glittery big letters on the cover of my journal. Then I lie down to ponder the big questions. Eventually I decide that life is very mysterious but that I must live it with as much brilliance as possible. I rummage under my bed and haul out the ripped poster of Jakob. I've been avoiding Jakob because I'm not proud of the fact that I attacked him and ripped his nose. I try to mend the ragged tear with sticky tape but the paper wrinkles and he ends up looking worse.

Jakob, I'm sorry. I didn't mean the bit about no one liking your music. You're the best songwriter and guitar player I know. I was just totally pissed off with everything and you were there to cop it. I can't get angry and yell at my mother because she'd crumble into a heap. If I throw a wobbly at Mel she might ditch me because now she has Toby. I don't have a father. My aunties and uncles live far away or else they're totally messed up themselves. I don't want to upset Grandpa Joseph so sometimes there's no one I can really talk to.

poetry of the sheets

Summer is drifting to an end. The lawns are scratchy brown, the evenings are getting cooler. It's a melancholy time of year. A time of loss and leaving, of things slipping away. Our garden is abundant with blowsy yellow roses, past their best, collapsing into piles of petals, leaving only dusty stem.

Here I am. Me. Georgia. These are gloomy times, my friend. My mother has been acting grumpy, snappish, peevish and pooped. She regrets her imperfect mother behaviour and tries to be friendly, but things are tricky between us. My mother needs a holiday. I need a life.

I should be writing my Media Studies essay right now but I can't get interested in the topic. The stupid thing was due on Friday but I was granted a special extension till Monday. Tomorrow. Yerk!

What are the main thematic issues dealt with in the work of Pedro Almodóvar? Has the way Almodóvar explores his themes remained constant throughout his career?

To be honest, I don't know and I don't care. It is the world's dumbest topic, and the dumbest thing is that I chose it myself. Mum comes in and asks how it's going. I say I'm making good progress but she knows I'm bullshitting.

'Do you need some more bum glue?' This is an ancient joke of ours — we never get tired of it.

things you either

'Yes please. I could do with several tubs.' She leaves. I yawn. Tra la la. What shall I do with my one and only glorious life?

I rearrange my coloured pencils, file a raggedy fingernail. I trawl the internet, and discover a superb site called Falling Fools, featuring impressive base-jumping loonies, who wander the world in search of high structures from which they hurl themselves. Watching such physical exertion makes me sleepy, although the guys are total hotties. There's something almost mystical about a young Austrian called Dirk wearing only a pair of shorts and a big grin. I take a squiz at the Rock Bitches site and send a few mean thoughts to Hayley and Fifi when I see their skinny arses on my screen. If I can't be with Jakob, why should they have the pleasure? Soon my guilt sends me back to my essay.

Almodóvar's films show great affection for his characters, I write. Then I pick a few fragments of glue from the edge of my desk and stare out the window, admiring the soft silvery sunset evening, until I notice the neighbour's spaniel doing a poo on our lawn. I stick my head out and yell at her. She gives me a furtive satisfied glance, then disappears through a hole in the hedge. The poo remains.

The phone rings. It's Adrian. He's lost his folder and can't remember the required essay length.

'Seven hundred and fifty words.'

'Bugger. I was hoping it was five hundred.'

I remind him it was due in on Friday, which cheers him even further. We discuss our topics. He's chosen a thematic study of *High Fidelity*, mainly because his fave actor is Jack Black. We talk movies for a minute, then run out of steam.

'Might as well get back into it.'

'Yeah, I guess.'
'See you at school.'
'Bye.'

❤

A key theme of Almodóvar's work is sexual identity. Ironic really. I'm fifteen years old and I'm writing an essay about something I have little experience of. However, miraculously, I cobble together some ideas that make sense. It's now three minutes past midnight. Splash my face. Scrub my teeth. Drop my clothes on the floor. Crawl into bed. Planet Dream, here comes Georgia.

❤

I spend lunchtime by myself the next day because Mel has orchestra practice. I sprawl out in the shade and eat my tomato sandwiches. My solitude is interrupted by a familiar voice on the other side of the hedge. It's Poppy. I'm listening with interest, having nothing better to do.

'Thank God it's lunchtime. We just had PE and Marilyn Erlich fainted. Mrs Ryan made us jog around the field while she took Marilyn to the sick bay, then she didn't come back for ages. I'm exhausted from all that running. Must have burned off heaps of calories though. And Eva, guess what Lauren just told me? You know how she and Rick Sturgess used to be an item, but then he ditched her? Well, now she's going out with Dylan, Rick's older brother, the one who sells wind chimes at the markets.'

I'm waiting for Eva to burst forth with a deluge of Oh My Gods, but she doesn't answer.

'Are you okay, Eva? Whassup?' Poppy obviously didn't expect silence in response to her fascinating tale.

things you either

'Hunter broke up with me.'

'No way. You're kidding, right?'

'Yeah right, Poppy. Big joke.'

'Oh my God! Why?'

'I don't want to talk about it, okay?'

'Are you sure? It might help?'

'Nothing's going to help. It's over, all right?'

'Okay. It's up to you.'

More silence. Then Eva changes her mind. Her voice is thin and trembly.

'Yesterday we hooked up after school, like we always do. Hunter said he wanted a coffee so we went to Starfish. We ordered, right, then he told me it was over. He didn't give a reason.'

'What did you say?'

'What *could* I say? We sat there awkwardly, waiting for the coffee, which took forever. Hunter was so nervous he spilled his down his front. Then he split.'

'Jeez, Eva, you guys seemed to have such a good thing going.'

'Yeah, well, it can't have been that good. I'm really pissed at him, to be honest. Anyway, I don't want to talk about it any more.'

❤

Oh my God. Oh my God. Oh my God.

I'm sitting bolt upright now, my mind a whirlwind of confusion.

What I should feel is *Poor Eva.*

What I actually feel is W*owie Zowie Ripptiddly Yaya!!!*

Hunter and Georgia. The movie. Titles in gold on black, border of stars and hearts. Cut to shot of me, looking good, holding hands with Hunter, who wears a suntan and royal blue satin boxers. We're on the verandah of our beach shack, listening to *White Dove Love* by Natural Affinity belting out down and dirty in the summer breeze.

My wild hope that perhaps I've got a chance with Hunter is rapidly followed by a parade of doubts. I am lumpy and chunky. I have the face of a peasant, full as a moon. He's as likely to fall in love with me as snow is to fall on Uluru at Christmas. Yet I spend the afternoon happily scribbling foolish roses on the last page of my homework notebook. What harm can it possibly do?

❦

I stroll out the school gate, crazy happy, and run into Adrian.

'Hiya, Georgia. I've been waiting for you. Mel said she didn't think you'd left yet. I wondered if you guys wanted to come to Chocolate Fish on Sunday afternoon to check out the food?'

'I work Sunday, but I finish at three. Can Mel make it?'

'Yeah, she's into it. Toby's coming as well.'

It didn't seem right to say no, even though when I finish work I'm generally so tired I go straight home to crash. So I smile feebly, which Adrian takes as a yes.'

'I work at New World in the city, near the bus depot. What bus should I get?'

'My dad's office is near there. He often works Sundays but he usually goes to the café for his afternoon caffeine fix. We could pick you up outside at three o'clock.'

'Make it ten past because it takes a while for me to sign out and get changed.'

Adrian goes away grinning. I'm grinning too, but for

things you either

quite a different reason. I'm not watching where I'm going and trip over my shoe, but who cares? Hunter no longer loves Eva, so ya ya ya!

Jobs that haven't YET been invented

leaf polisher in the botanic gardens
person who tells people their cat got run over
travel agent who organises bad holidays,
     so your life seems better when you get home
co-ordinator of 12-step program for ageing rock stars
     who can't give up young blonde girls

Great excuses for not doing my homework

My uncle died
My pen died
My dog died
I died
It's against my religion
Shit happens. Miracles take a little longer.

Excuses I could have made to Adrian

I'll be too tired
I'd rather eat ants
I have an appointment with my psychiatrist
I don't travel in cars, only balloons
It's against my religion
My uncle died
My dog died
I died
I don't want to

Bugger it, I've already said yes. I might as well go.

☙

On Sunday I make a special effort with my appearance. I'm not a hundred percent sure I want to go, but I don't want to look rank, either. I plunder Mum's cosmetics for bronze foundation and terracotta eye shadow, put my hair up with a tortoiseshell clip and take my purple silky shirt. I can get changed after work and the shirt looks okay with my black pants. I spend so long getting ready that I miss the bus, but Mum is off to sing wildly with the Wild Women so I score a lift to work.

'Is this a date with Adrian, then?' Mum enquires as we drive through the suburbs.

'No way. I've already told you, we're just going to check out the food, get some ideas for camp.'

My mother doesn't answer, but she sneaks a glance to see if my face reveals any further information. I stare out the window, reverting to my childhood game of counting things, such as funky letterboxes and white cats. I hide a tiny smile. There are some things a girl wants to keep for herself. Which is bizarre, seeing I don't really want to go and I'm not that fussed about Adrian. At least I didn't want to go, but now maybe I do? Even though Adrian is just a school mate, he's male and he seems to want my company. Or is he just doing this to be helpful about camp food? I am confused but that's just how it is.

'See you, petal.'

'*Ciao*, Mum. Have fun.'

'Sure you can get home okay?'

'Yeah, no worries. If I can't get a lift home I'll get the bus. Or ring you.'

'Righty oh. Take care.'

※

things you either

The morning passes uneventfully. At first there aren't any customers so I compose a list in my head to write down later. It's one of my best lists ever.

Things you can't see
    Your mother's wedding day
    Your bones
    A wish leaving your heart
    The next word you will write
    Snow before it falls
    The tooth fairy
    The buried penguin of Antarctica

By mid-morning things are busy. Supermarkets are great places for observing the human race. My most interesting sighting is a bleach-blonde mother with a bleach-blonde daughter. They're almost identical, dressed in matching blue jeans and lace tops. Only the mother's skin gives her away. It's wrinkly and crocodiley, especially around her eyes and neck, as if she's been left out in the sun to dry. Kind of like a sun-dried tomato.

In my haste to get ready I didn't eat breakfast, so by noon I'm hungry. I grab a tub of potato salad from the deli counter, half a dozen big juicy strawberries and a juice, and I take them through Check-out 7. Zoe doesn't scan the berries, just hands them across to me with a wink. I'd rather she hadn't done that but it seems weird to say anything, so I don't. I'm not going to waste valuable eating time with moral indignation. There's only one other person in the lunch room. It's Hunter, munching a pie and swigging chocolate milk. His big feet are propped up on a chair and he's listening to his walkman as well as scribbling something intently on a piece of A4 paper. When he sees me he takes off his headphones and gives me that heart-melting smile.

'Hey Georgia.'

'Hey Hunter.'

For one ghastly minute I fear I have Echo Disease. What if I'm unable to stop repeating everything he says?

How are you? How are you?

I'm fine. I'm fine.

Stop doing that. Stop doing that.

I pull myself back from Loopyville.

'Who are you listening to, then?'

'Bored Gordon. They're a New Zealand band. I love 'em. They're so grunty they're dirty.'

'What sort of music do you like?'

'House, techno at the more mellow end. My stepfather has some sixties stuff that's pretty fine. Jimmy Hendrix, Janis Joplin, The Doors.'

'What are you writing?'

'A poem.'

'Really? Can I read it?'

He looks at me doubtfully. 'It's fairly strange.'

'Strange is good. I can do strange. I'd love to see it.'

'It's very messy. I doubt whether you'd be able to read my writing.'

'You read it to me, then.'

'Nah.'

This word is followed by a very awkward silence. Neither of us is sure what to do next so we concentrate on our food. The potato salad isn't great. Hunter wipes pie crumbs off his shirt and hesitantly begins to speak.

'If you're really up for strange, here goes. I've been

things you either

reading a book called *The Unbearable Lightness of Being*. The part I read last night was about humans and their relationship to shitting. Also, I've spent my entire morning unpacking rolls of toilet paper, just me and a whole aisle of fluffy products. It suddenly boggled me, so many styles, so many patterns. Made me think about what a weird culture we live in, and what a strange relationship we have with the things we buy. So I wrote this poem. It's not finished yet.'

I can't believe it. This beautiful boy is about to read me a poem. I close my eyes and listen.

I choose
the pure soft luxury of silk.
Hypo-allergenic, triple-strength,
embossed with a delicate design
of crimson petals on palest pink four-ply.

Cream constellations of suns and moons,
symphonies of white heather, silver stars,
bouquets of yellow daisies and mauve tulips,
umbrellas, suns, little blue penguins, lurid green starfish.
Ultra-strong, ultra-soft.
Scented with lavender, gardenia, peach blossom, delicate rose.

So many choices,
leave me
wandering the toilet paper aisle
in constipated indecision
wondering if
by some remarkable feat of human evolution
my arse has grown a nose and eyes.

He looks up, grinning.

'Maybe I should say bum, instead of arse?'

'No way. It's brilliant just as it is.'

❦

We gaze happily at each other. Yay for poetry and yay for my amazing feeling of contentment. For once in my life I feel as if I'm in the right place at the right time with the absolutely right person.

I reach for a strawberry, but I don't want to put it in my mouth. When Zoe gave them to me I felt uneasy, now I feel worse.

'These strawberries are stolen goods,' I say. Hunter raises a puzzled eyebrow.

'When I came through Zoe's check-out she scammed the strawberries for me, and I feel weird about eating them.'

'How easily scanning becomes scamming,' Hunter says sympathetically. Whew. I was worried he would think me odd.

'Yeah. My mother reckons stealing is bad karma. I do nick flowers sometimes, though.'

'Roadsideia.'

'What?'

'That's what my aunty calls flowers that lean over hedges and ask to be taken home. I'm with you, though, about not nicking stuff from shops. What goes around comes around, and all that. It makes sense.'

'Mmm,' I reply, staring mournfully at the strawberries.

'We could take them back,' says Hunter. 'Reverse stealing. Let's return them.'

'You're on.' We sneak into the store on our softest feet. Past the dairy products, past the chilled juices, past the enticing displays of chocolate biscuits.

things you either

Hunter does a silly walk, hamming it up like a complete looper. I'm finding it difficult not to laugh out loud and he knows it, so he creates more silly steps, which look hilarious because of his lanky legs. We almost trip over each other. He is so near I can smell him. He smells good, a clean sweaty boy fragrance.

There's only one person in the fruit and vegetable aisle, a woman selecting mushrooms. She doesn't take any notice of us. Perhaps she's dreaming about the mushroom soufflé she wants to make for dinner. Anyhow, her back is turned and we tiptoe towards the strawberries. Just as Hunter replaces the last one Mrs J swoops around the corner. She halts, regarding us with suspicion. 'What are you two up to? You mustn't eat any of those berries, you know. They're export quality.'

'We weren't, honestly,' I say. I sound guilty, even though I'm innocent.

'For real,' says Hunter. 'Look, no sign of strawberry.' He opens wide and swivels his head so that Mrs J is looking into his mouth. She's so unnerved by his odd behaviour that she turns and hurries away. 'Well, whatever you were up to, don't!' is her parting shot.

'Yeah, no worries,' Hunter mumbles. He turns to me. 'What are you doing after work?'

I'm not sure I've heard him right.

'Well, Mel and I are doing the food for camp. This afternoon we're going on a mission to suss out the menu at Chocolate Fish.'

'Cool. See ya.' Hunter smiles, but it's not his usual radiant grin. Before I can add anything, he ambles away.

Wait. Why? I'd rather do something with you. That's if you were going to ask me to.

Zoe is glaring at me, because she wants her break, so I reluctantly take up my position and get back to work.

take me to the chocolate fish

I didn't like the guy even before he spoke to me. Forty-something, sandy hair, pale speckled skin. Grey shirt. Polyester business pants with pleats. Huge set of keys dangling from his pocket. He struts up, aggressively thrusting an advertising brochure into my face.

'It says here Angus Brut is on sale for $8.95, but you don't have any. I drove all the way from the other side of the city specifically to get some. It just isn't good enough!'

'I'm sorry but there's been a huge demand for it. We should have more tomorrow.'

'That's no use to me. I made a special trip here, I already told you that.' His eyes are squinty with rage. Why is he being so nasty? Blasting my arse won't produce any of his stupid bubbly.

'I'm sorry about that. Unfortunately there isn't anything I can do, but if you'd like to talk to my supervisor she's over there at the service desk.'

'Bloody disgraceful,' he mutters as he stomps off towards Mrs J.

Get a bit of perspective on this, you idiot. Millions of people on this planet don't even have drinking water. Furthermore, only losers with tiny dicks wear big jangly sets of keys like that!

Once I've got that off my chest I feel a little better, but not for long because an elderly customer knocks over her eggs as she fumbles for her purse and one of the eggs cracks open.

things you either

'No worries,' I say, trying to wipe sticky slimy egg off my belt and managing to smear it everywhere. Finally I have to ask for help. A crabby Mrs J zaps it for me with her magic spray bottle. At the far end of the store I can see Hunter, his tall back, those lovely curls. Far away and seriously not mine.

☜

It's been all downhill since lunchtime and by three o'clock I'm well ready to leave. I nip into the ladies, neaten my hair, change into my purple top. Not bad for a basket case, I reassure myself. Adrian is standing outside, waiting for me.

'Hiya.'

'Hi, Georgia. Dad's waiting at his office, just around the corner.'

'Sweet.' We stroll off, but something makes me glance back. Oh no. I don't believe it. Hunter is standing outside, watching us. He stares at me, raises a quizzical eyebrow. Going somewhere with Mel? Yeah, right. He shrugs and walks away.

'Shit!' I say, loudly.

'Pardon me?'

'I've had the most horrible afternoon.' There's no way I can tell Adrian what's happened. 'Let's not even go there.'

'Here's Dad's office.'

'Cool.'

Adrian's father has a client with him who's coming for coffee, so Adrian and I hop in the back. It's a very classy car: the latest model Volkswagen. I feel dire but decide that the best way to survive is to ask heaps of questions. By the time we pull up outside Chocolate Fish I know the following about Adrian.

Star Sign – Sagittarius
Fave TV show – Dark Angel
Fave Computer Game – Half-Life
Siblings – None
Parents – Zelda and Nigel.
　　She runs Chocolate Fish, he's a stockbroker.
Countries lived in – Australia, New Zealand,
　　Switzerland, Hong Kong
Best Friends – Ben and Martin
Sport – Basketball
Fave Band – The White Stripes

Adrian is happy to talk about himself so I listen, but only with one ear and none of my heart. All I can think about is Hunter. I can't get past the image of him standing by himself, watching us. Trying to pretend he didn't give a shit. But he did. I saw it in his hurt eyes.

By the time we pull up outside the café I've made up my mind about Adrian. He's an okay person but he'll never be the love of my life. Not that he has actually applied for the position or anything. He's friendly, okay looking, easy to talk to but lacks the Oomph Factor. Face it girl, Hunter is the one.

Things I like about HUNTER
　　he's a strawberry returner
　　his golden-curls – I want to run my fingers
　　　　through his hair
　　I can talk to him
　　we laugh at the same stuff
　　he smells of clean sweat and apples
　　he writes mad poetry
　　I feel happy to be me when I'm around him

It'll be okay, I reassure myself. I'll see Hunter at work next Saturday. I'll explain about the mix up, tell him that I really was going to Chocolate Fish with Mel.

✿

'Hiya!' Mel and Toby are outside, waving. It's famous, this place. The café's on one side of the road and the tables are on the other, perched on a little jetty beside the sea. The wait-people scoot across the road on roller skates, carrying trays balanced with lattes and macchiatos.

Adrian introduces us to Zelda, who is a very funky mother. Red lippie, ultra short silver hair, tight jeans, black t-shirt, an armada of silver jewellery.

'Call me Zee, okay? Good to meet you guys at last. Adrian's told me all about you, especially you, Georgia. Come on, I'll show you the kitchen.'

I don't know if this woman is wired on caffeine or if she's just a natural-born raver, but Zee doesn't stop talking the whole time we're there. She instructs the kitchen-hand to show us all the food, gives us samples to taste, jots down a list of suppliers, orders the barista to make us free coffees, asks heaps of stuff but never leaves any space for us to answer. She just lets the questions hang and powers onwards. Luckily her mobile rings so the four of us finish our coffees and chill for a bit, sitting at a table by the water.

'Sorry about my mother. She's pretty full-on.'

'Nah, she's good.' I say. 'Must be a bit hard to keep up with at times, though.'

'Tell me about it. Anyhow, you guys want to come back to my place and hang for a while?'

'Mel and I might peel off now if that's okay with you,

man? Have a quiet wander along to the end of the bay, catch the bus home later.'

'Yeah, for sure. How about you, Georgia? Dad's keen to get going. He's dropping me off, then heading back to work.'

I really feel like going home and crashing but…

'Well, I could come over for a little while, but I need to be home by six. I have huge amounts of homework waiting for me.'

'For sure.'

❤

I'm reluctant to say goodbye to Mel and Toby. The four of us doing the café thing was fine, but being alone with Adrian feels odd, though it's too late to get out of it now. I'm worn out by the Manic Mama experience and I can't think of any more questions so we just sit in the back seat and drive along listening to David Gray on the groovy sound system. Adrian's house is impressive: a sleek mansion on the edge of a cliff. Nigel pulls up next to a silver BMW, waves goodbye and backs down the drive like a demon. I follow Adrian onto a wooden viewing platform that overlooks a slender velvet lawn and a lap pool. Beyond that the city sprawls out, a moving map of tiny buildings and snaking freeways. Adrian disappears into a huge space, bare except for three black leather couches, a crystal chandelier and a grand piano.

'Wow. Swanky.'

'Yeah, I guess. I don't actually like this house much. I preferred the one in Hong Kong. It was simpler. This one is over the top.'

'Yeah, well, I'm impressed.'

'Want a drink? Juice? Coke?'

'Juice would be good.'

We take our drinks into Adrian's room. It's tidier than my bedroom will ever be, and I tell him so.

'That's only because our cleaner comes on Saturdays. I wish we didn't have her, either. I'd like my mess left alone. When she's been I can never find anything.' He gives me an apologetic look.

Don't worry. I don't care if you're rich. A crass thing I decide not to say.

Now that he has me at his house, Adrian seems shy. Me too. I sit on his bed. My only other options are the computer chair, on which he's perched, or the red bean bag. No way I'm sitting on that. I always feel particularly fat when I struggle out of a bean bag. Adrian shows me some of his favourite computer games and plays me the latest White Stripes CD. I'm restless. I'd like to say 'What time do the buses go?' but we only just got there. We scratch around for things to talk about, finally settling on the reliable topic of the camp menu.

'I still don't know quite what Mel's going to eat. Flatbread wraps will be okay if she leaves out the tuna. Being a vegan makes life complicated. I'd hate to miss out on the cheesy frittata, but Mel's convictions are very strong. Hey, it was superb of your mother to give us the recipe for that fruity slice thing.'

'Yeah, that one's foolproof. Quick, too. I made some for my basketball wind-up.'

'Do you like cooking, then?'

'Yeah, I do. The food in Hong Kong is so good. I learned quite a few Cantonese dishes from our cook.'

'It must have been amazing, living there.'

'Yeah, I loved it.'

'What about Switzerland?'

'I don't really remember it that much. We left when I was two.'

'How come you came back here?'

'My father's job was extremely stressful, and my mother got bored doing the expat wife thing. You've met Zee – she operates on high voltage.' I grin. Adrian goes over to his shelves and brings a small carved statue to show me.

'People think this fat guy is Buddha, but he isn't. He was a happy monk, so the story goes. Children loved him, he used to give them sour plum sweets. It's supposed to be lucky to rub his belly.'

'Cool.'

Adrian perches awkwardly on the edge of the bed beside me. I smell Coca-Cola on his breath and I realise oh no, he's going to try and kiss me. Which he does.

Without thinking I half-turn away, which means Adrian's lips land beside my mouth, rather than on it, but he perseveres. His arm swings around my shoulders and he pulls me towards him, seeking out my mouth with his and planting a rubbery kiss. I don't reciprocate, so he stops. Neither of us says anything. He stumbles back to his computer desk – won't look in my direction.

'I'm sorry Georgia, but I've liked you for ages. I thought you felt the same about me…'

'Why?'

'Well, you're friendly to me, and you came to the café today and then you came back here…'

'I didn't mean to give you the wrong signals. I'm friendly to most people. Doesn't mean I want to be kissed by them.'

things you either

'I get that now.'

'I should go home.'

'You don't have to.'

'Nah, really, I should.'

We wait at the bus stop in silence. As the bus pulls up, Adrian plucks up courage to speak.

'Don't be pissed off at me, Georgia.'

'No harm done. See you in class. Bye.'

♥

There's no one on the bus but me. I'm so tired I feel ill. I'm gutted about Hunter. I feel terrible about Adrian. Today has been the pits.

When I get home Mum and Penny are playing a drunken game of Scrabble at the kitchen table. There's not much left in the bottle of red wine, but two slices of a large pizza remain in the Dino's box.

'Hey, sweetie. How was your day?'

'Fine.'

'We left you some pizza, and there's other stuff in the fridge, rocket and tomatoes and things.'

'It's okay. I had something to eat at the café. Actually, I'm not feeling particularly great. I think I'll just have a shower and hop into bed.'

'What sort of not great, love? Tummy?' Mum looks up, concerned.

'Yeah, tummy and a bit of a headache,' I lie. 'Nothing major. No need to fuss. Who's winning?'

'Penny, but not for long. I'm about to trash her.'

'Yeah, right. In your dreams, vixen.' Now Penny is checking me out as well. 'You do look a bit pale, Georgia. Shall I make you a hot drink or something?'

'If you're having one, a cup of tea would be nice.' I head upstairs, keen to avoid any further questioning. It's not until I'm safely tucked up under my quilt that I realise it wasn't a lie. I do feel sick. Nauseous, hot and headachy. My eyes hurt, too. By the time Penny comes up with a mug of tea, I'm so nearly asleep that I can only manage a few sips before I'm out like a light.

❣

I have a very strong constitution. Usually when I feel sick it doesn't last: I go to bed and after a good night's sleep I wake up feeling fine. But not this time. I'm not even sure if I am asleep or awake but I decide that I'm awake, because I can hear Mum yelling at me.

Get up! Get cracking, Georgia! It's late! Didn't you hear your alarm?

No, I did not. I've been asleep forever, drowning in disturbing dreams. I start to get up but my limbs won't work properly. I feel as if I've been drugged.

'Mum,' I call, but my voice won't come out right. When I hear her coming past my door I call out again.

'Mum, I'm crook.' At first she doesn't believe me.

'Come on, get up. Don't pull your Mondayitis trick on me again, Georgia.'

'I promise, Mum, this is for real. My eyes hurt, my throat's raw and I'm all weak and woozy.'

'Sounds like the flu. Hang on, I'll get dressed and we'll take your temperature.'

Once I sit up I feel marginally less like cottonwool girl.

'I've got a big meeting this morning but your temperature's up, so stay in bed. I'll call you at lunchtime to see how you are.' My mother looks somewhat crap herself, tired and anxious. I feel bad, as if I'm just one more problem in her life. 'No worries, Mum.'

❤

I sit propped up in bed in my faded pyjamas. I feel dire. I'm feverish, and everything aches: my throat, my head, my bones. I'm not hungry, most unusual for me, so I snuggle down and snooze off again. When Mum phones I tell her I'm still feeling dreadful so she arranges a doctor's appointment and tells me to be ready at three. Around noon I drag myself out of bed. I'm weak and sweaty. I have a shower, put on my old dressing gown and go downstairs. I eat some yoghurt, which is soft and cool on my throat, and wash down some painkillers with weak black tea. I sit in the garden and write.

Things you either love or hate
anchovies • The Simpsons • The Olsen twins beer • cute fluffy poodles • pink carnations Britney Spears • coriander • socks • rainy days

important questions
Will I get another chance with Hunter?
Why is the world so f*cked up?
Can my aunt and uncle's marriage be saved?
Is it normal to worry so much about other people's troubles?
Will my mother ever get over my father and find a nice partner?
What if she finds a horrible partner?
Will God punish me because I hate Eva?
(Don't let her do her strange blonde magic & get Hunter back again...)

things that go up & down
> umbrellas
> pogo sticks
> elevators
> stairs
> escalators
> the Dow Jones index
> my level of happiness
> boy eyes, checking you out

things i like about myself
> *I am honest*
> *My hair (sometimes)*

I feel too ill to write any more so I sprawl on the couch, flick on the telly and watch Oprah. Four drab suburban mothers in saggy tracksuits are given makeovers. They emerge wearing big hair, high heels, short skirts and heaps of make-up. To me they look plastic, but maybe it's because I feel so revolting. My face is swollen, my body aches and there's a blob of dried yoghurt on my sleeve. Turn off telly. Pick at yoghurt with fingernail in a dispirited fashion. Wish was dead.

❦

Mum rushes in at the appointed time to take me to the doctor. Stephen is young, balding and smiley. He resembles a cheery big brother rather than a GP. He pokes and prods me, asks heaps of questions, then says Mum had better come in.

'So, Georgia. What have you been up to lately? Kissed any nice boys? I'm going to do a blood test, but I think you have glandular fever.'

things you either

I stare at him, aghast. Then I burst into tears, because Adrian has given me glandular fever.

❤

The next ten minutes are very confusing for us all. To cut a long story short, I fess up about Adrian. Mum is appalled, mainly because I can't stop crying. My tears pour out in a salty deluge. Mum drags out the counselling word again, which shits me. Can't I even cry without being labelled bonkers? Stephen tries to take us seriously but can't stop smirking. He explains that the incubation period for glandular fever is around six weeks, so my illness has nothing to do with what happened yesterday. He asks whether I kissed or was kissed by any boys about six weeks ago? I say no, no, no, definitely no. Then I sob a bit more, with self-pity, because Adrian is the only boy who's ever kissed me. Stephen offers me a tissue, and asks about sick friends. Do I have any? Yeah, plenty, I think, but not the sort of sick you're talking about.

'I can't remember any of my friends being ill,' I tell him.

'Well, think hard about this before you answer. Did you share food or drink with anyone at school in the last few months?'

'Um...only Mel, and she hasn't been sick.'

Stephen looks puzzled and waits patiently, either for me to stop blubbing or for a new sensible question to arrive in his brain. All of a sudden I have an Ah-Ha moment. Or rather an Oh-No moment. My first day of work at the supermarket. Tammy fainting. A chocolate thickshake on a hot day. Too rich, too sweet, too cold, too thick. That's how I got glandular fever.

'I'll organise a blood test but I'm pretty sure I'm on to it.

The bad news is that sometimes the initial symptoms are the mildest, so things may get worse before they get better. In your case it seems to have kicked in with a vengeance. Hopefully this will be the worst you'll feel.'

'But what can I do about it?'

'Not much, I'm afraid. There's no cure for glandular fever; it just has to run its course. Get plenty of rest, keep your liquids up, sit in the sunshine each day. Get a little exercise but don't overdo it. Take life gently and listen to your body. It's really a matter of doing everything you can to get your immune system powered up, which speeds the healing process. Take codeine for the aches and pains. A multi-vitamin tablet won't hurt, and I'll order a full blood picture, in case your iron is low.'

'When will I be better?' I whimper. 'When can I go back to school and to work?'

'Not for a few weeks at least. Let's see how you go. There are no definitive answers where glandular fever is. Progress pretty much depends on the individual. I'll see you again in a fortnight, unless things get a lot worse, in which case bring her back sooner, okay?' Mum nods.

'Here's an information sheet, and I'll write a medical certificate to send to your school. Come now, Georgia, why so gloomy? A few weeks at home chilling out, surely that's not so bad?'

Don't adults understand anything? This guy just doesn't get it.

It's like this, Doctor Cheerful. I won't be able to see Hunter or explain to him that I wasn't sneaking off with Adrian. By the time we see each other he'll have forgotten my name. I'm going to miss out on camp, get way behind on my schoolwork, and be bored shitless at home alone.

things you either

Maybe for months. I have the energy level of a squashed flea. God has sprinkled iron filings on the raw tissue of my throat. My head has a team of black dudes with big shoes jumping around inside it. I don't see how things could get any worse.

As we drive home Mum starts freaking.

'This is terrible. The timing couldn't be worse. I'll try to arrange some time off but it's tricky because Natalie's away. I could ask, though...'

'Don't worry. I'll be fine. You can bring me some library books. I've got my journal. School will send me assignments. It'll be okay.' I wish I didn't have to reassure her. I'm ill and irritable; I don't want to have to prop her up.

❤

Trying to be cheerful is all very well, but having glandular fever is no fun at all.

Firstly, as Stephen predicted, my symptoms worsened. My glands swelled up so that my face resembled a rubbery pumpkin. My whole body ached and my throat hurt so much that I couldn't chew. Painkillers took the edge off things and Mum whizzed up concoctions of juice, yoghurt and spirulina so I didn't starve to death. I wasn't allowed visitors, unless they'd already had glandular fever. Mrs Jakovich sounded frazzled when I phoned to say I couldn't work for at least three weeks but sent me a glittery Get Well card with tulips on, which was sweet. School, on the other hand, posted me a whole lot of assignments, which I couldn't face doing. The days passed slowly. I slept a lot, watched endless junk TV, and wrote a list or two, but everything felt lacklustre.

❤

Mel rang every night, which was great, until she dropped her bombshell.

'School is crap without you, Georgia.'

'Who are you hanging out with?'

'No one really. Toby's getting a bit clingy. It's driving me nuts, actually, so I ate lunch by myself today. I'm doing a fruit cleanse, so it was just me and an apple and a bottle of pear juice. I sat by Eva on the bus on the way home, or rather she sat by me. She was wearing black fishnet stockings and trainers with her school uniform. She'd put the stockings on at the bus stop. They looked kind of strange but good, in an only-Eva-could-pull-this-off way. Anyway, she couldn't stop talking about that guy from Metro College, the one who works at the supermarket with you. Hunter? Apparently they're getting back together again. She's obsessed with him. Wouldn't shut up about it.'

I felt as if I'd died and gone straight to hell without passing Go, but I kept my voice neutral. I'd never quite got around to telling Mel about my stupid crush on Hunter.

'Are you sure?'

'Yep. Apparently he ditched her without giving a reason and she rang him last night and asked him to reconsider. He didn't say he would but he didn't say no. They're going to hook up after school tomorrow to talk. It sounds promising. Eva's rapt.'

'F*ck,' I mumble.

'What?'

I quickly changed the topic by asking a boring homework question. When I got off the phone I made myself a hot chocolate but even the frothy sweetness didn't help. Any feeble chance I had with Hunter was gone. I thought that was as low as things could go but I was wrong:

things you either

things were about to go from bad to terrible to absolutely rank.

⚘

On Friday night Mum says she has a treat for me.

'What?' I ask expectantly.

'Gilda's back and she's coming over. She's been tested and she has the antibody, even though she hasn't actually had glandular fever. Some kids are exposed to it in childhood and develop a natural resistance.'

'Cool.'

♥

I'm glad to see Gilda. Staying with Sooze has changed her. Her long blonde hair has been styled into a textured bob and she's looking slinky in an old dress of Sooze's: turquoise with roses. She tells me about snorkelling and picking mangoes and learning salsa dancing. Her voice is different, more lively. She doesn't seem as pale any more.

Auntie Joy has sent over a basket of goodies: mango juice, jasmine soap and some glossy magazines. Gilda and I watch a *Friends* rerun and have a good giggle at Joey trying to teach Ross how to talk dirty.

'Tell me more about the tropical north. Entertain me with wondrous tales,' I plead, when the show's over.

'It was good. I mean Sooze is kind of nuts but she's fun.'

'Yeah, not like Mum. She lost fun some time ago, I'm afraid.'

'Sooze mentioned that, actually. We were talking about families, about how people turn out and Sooze told me...' Gilda tails off. She has a funny look on her face. Guilty, almost.

'Go on,' I urge.

'Nah, probably best I don't, actually.'

'You've got me intrigued now. If my mother has a fascinating secret I'd love to hear it.'

'Well,' says Gilda, slowly and doubtfully. 'Actually, it wasn't about your mother. It was about your father, but I really don't think we should be having this conversation.'

'Whatever it is, I think I have a right to know. I lost my father when I was four. Don't I at least deserve to know about him?'

'Yeah, I suppose so, but I don't want to upset you. And I don't want to get in the shit.'

'Please, Gilda. Tell me.'

'Well, all right. Your dad wasn't the perfect person your mother makes him out to be. He had a gambling problem. Huge debts.'

'Gambling debts. No way!'

'Yeah, he liked to bet on the horses apparently, but it got out of control. In the beginning his parents bailed him out, but then they stopped. Grandad tried to get your mother to leave your father at one stage because things were so dodgy. The way Sooze tells it, your father was a nice guy but weak. She reckons your mum has forgotten all his faults and is stuck in the past.'

'Wow.' I'm gob smacked. I don't know what to say. Gilda sort of panics after that. She says she has a bit of a headache, and would I mind if she didn't stay late?

'No problem. I'm fading a bit myself. I'll read the magazines you brought. Thanks for coming over, Gildz.'

I'm stunned by what I've learned, but I can't face thinking about it. Blank it out and deal with it later. I get comfy on my pillows and begin flicking through the glossies, losing myself in recipes for Moroccan food and wonderful photos of Southern India. Penny's told me lots about India. She lived there in her twenties, still wears bangles and bindis. I check out my horoscope, which says I'm about to have a challenging incident that will change my life. Yeah, right. I pick up the *Rolling Stone.* The White Stripes, The Brunettes and the Sugarcubes all have new albums out. Music to get trashed to, the reviewer notes. Then I turn the page and spot an article about Natural Affinity.

TOUR CANCELLED:

The Heavy Price of Life on the Road

Thousands of contemporary music lovers will be disappointed to learn of the break-up of funk band Natural Affinity. Two members, Jakob Larsen and Fifi Tarrant, have been admitted to the Betty Ford clinic, confirming recent rumours about their shared battle with heroin addiction. Apparently the third member of the band, Hayley Tarrant, is now living in Southern California at a yoga ashram. 'Music has been my life for too long. I need to restore some balance,' Tarrant is reported to have told close friend Sheena Leena, lead singer of girl band Jittery. A spokesman from Natural Affinity's record company, John Gilbert, says there are no plans for the group to re-form. 'Due to personal difficulties all three musicians need time to attend to health issues and to recharge their creative batteries.' Gilbert offered his apologies to the multitude of Natural Affinity fans who were eagerly awaiting the May Day Bash. The lead act is now rumoured to be Salmonella

Dub, although this is yet to be confirmed. John Gilbert urges fans to keep on buying the music. 'Miracles do happen. Perhaps in the future we'll see the band back on their feet, but for now, play those CDs guys, and remember to keep it real.'

❤

F*ck. F*ck. F*ck. No wonder they were so goddamn skinny! I am furious. I drag out the poster, rip it into little pieces and chuck them into my rubbish bin. Jakob, how could you, you loser? I blast the shit out of him for ten minutes. All right Jakob, I say. Get yourself together. Find out who you are and what life is like without a needle in your arm. Then write me a song.

❤

I push the information about my father to the back of my brain. It's huge. I can't deal with it. Mum seems to know that something's up. She keeps asking me if anything is the matter.

'I'm sick, for God's sake,' I say. 'Just leave me alone, can't you?'

I fall into a deep hole. Life doesn't seem worth living. Eva and Hunter are back together. Jakob turns out to be a junkie loser. There's no concert to look forward to, and I'm going to miss the stupid camp. I sleep a lot. I can't read for long because my eyes hurt. I don't feel like eating. Partly my sore throat, partly I just can't be bothered. Mum keeps the smoothies coming but she puts wheatgerm and brewer's yeast in, to build up my strength, so I refuse to drink them until she loses the healthy stuff. Sometimes I eat a bowl of vegie soup just to get her off my case. Mum hassles me into

things you either

going outside, reckons I need the fresh air. I sit in the garden in my pyjamas feeling sorry for myself. I feel like a half-sucked jube. Can't be bothered writing lists. Mel rings with big news. She's split up with Toby because she was finding him too needy. I'm surprised but not totally. Poor Toby: he'll be gutted. I don't ask about Eva and Hunter. My pride won't let me. I don't want Mel to know that Hunter meant anything.

⋆♥⋆

A few nights later Mel rings again.

'Guess what?'

Oh no, not guess what again.

'You got back with Toby?'

'Don't be ridiculous. He keeps phoning me but it's over.'

'So, what then?'

'I'm going to the movies with someone else.'

'Yeah? Who?'

'Hunter. He and Eva didn't get back together. She wanted to but he didn't, apparently. Did I forget to tell you that? Anyhow, she's devastated. And now he's asked *me* to the movies.'

My heart turns to ice, to lead, to fire. My head is about to explode. How could he? I mean, apart from anything else, they don't even know each other, or I didn't think they did.

'Some of the kids from Metro come to our Japanese class. I was sure I told you about that. Anyhow, Hunter and I started talking. We're going to see *Lost in Translation,* which is set in Tokyo. It's supposed to be really good.'

'Wow.'

'Yeah, I'm kind of excited. He's such a babe.'

'Indeed.'

'Georgia? Whassup? You sound strange.'

'Nothing.'

'Don't give me that. What's the matter?'

'If you must know, I had a bit of a thing for him.'

'Hunter? You're kidding! You never said anything.'

'Nah, well. What was the point? He was going out with Eva, apart from anything else.'

'You should've told me. We tell each other everything. This is crazy. Well, that's it then. I won't go.'

'Don't be silly. You have to go. It was just a stupid fantasy. Nah, go for it, Mel.'

'Really?'

'Yeah, for sure.'

❤

Even though I told Mel to go, it hurt that she gave in so readily. Friends are supposed to be loyal to each other, beyond anything else. Maybe my view is unreasonable but that's how I see it. I descend into a hard-edged world, accompanied by the seven dwarves: Slimy, Edgy, Lonely, Cranky, Murky, Shitty and Blobby. I stay in bed. I don't shower. My hair gets stringy and oily, I look disgusting. It freaks Mum out. I'm glad.

Great email addresses

whiteferret@htmail.com

friendlyfairy@....

Holdmypursewhileistealyourboyfriend@htmail.com

Boredom. Boredom. Boredom. My lists are shite. My hair is shite and my room is shite, big-time. My floor is littered with dirty clothes, the flowers that Penny brought me are

things you either

shrivelled and dead. The water in their clear glass vase is cloudy and green. It stinks. Life stinks. I'm sick of everything. Sick of myself, my crappy room and my crappy life. I'm really pissed off about Mel and Hunter, but what's the point of agonising about it. He likes her, not me. So that's that. I shall try to rise above it. Shit happens but life must go on.

One night Mum comes into my room and bollocks me about the load of washing I was supposed to do. She doesn't just complain and get out of my room, she goes on and on about it.

'Get over it! I forgot. I'm sorry, okay? I'll do it tomorrow, what difference does it make?' I begin doodling in my journal, hoping she'll buzz off, but she doesn't. She just keeps on coming.

'I'm worried about you. I really think you need to see a counsellor, Georgia.'

'I'm worried about me too. Everything's turned to custard since I got sick, but I don't want counselling. I'm not nuts, and I can work things out by myself.'

'I didn't say you were nuts.'

'You're insinuating it, each time you mention counselling. It implies that you don't trust me to find my own solutions. There's no need to worry about my comfort eating, by the way. I weighed myself this morning and I've lost four kilos. Look.'

I pull up my pyjama top to display my flattish tummy.

'That's wonderful,' says Mum. 'Good girl.'

Suddenly, with huge force, rage rises up in me from my dark depths. *Good girl.* Good grief. I'm not six years old! I'm sick of being treated like a child, of trying to please her. I'm tired of having to get it right. I can't handle her nagging, or her constant attempts to turn me into something I'm not.

'Yes. You can put it on your list of things to impress people with,' I say, sarcastically.

'I was only trying to be encouraging. No need to get shirty.'

'Oh no, we mustn't be shirty, must we? Nicey pie and full of bullshit is what we have to be around here, isn't it?'

'Georgia! What on earth's going on?'

'I'll tell you what's going on! You lay all this counsellor crap on me, when it's *you* that needs to sort yourself out. I know about Dad – you know, about his gambling. Why didn't you tell me? You can't face the truth, that's why. You'd rather live in your safe little world of lies. Well, I won't live there with you any more. '

My mother's face crumples and she starts to cry. I don't know what to do. My anger seeps away, leaving me clumsy and shy. I put an awkward arm round her shoulders.

'It's okay. Mum. It's good to cry. '

'Better bring the tissues, then.'

'For real. How about a cup of tea?'

'Yes. I could do with one.' She gives me a wobbly smile. 'I didn't know how to tell you. In the beginning, you were too little and once you were older, it felt too late. I wanted you to have good memories, instead of hard ones.'

'How bad was it, his gambling?'

'At first, it was manageable. He'd go to the races, and either win or lose, but only small amounts. Later, it got pretty devastating. We were in real financial trouble a lot of the time. He'd promise to stop, but he couldn't.'

'But you always loved him, didn't you?'

'Yes, I always did. But it's hard to love someone you can't rely on. I nearly left him once, the time he lost five thousand dollars on a sure thing.'

'Why didn't you?'

'He said he'd get help. He did stop, too, for a while. But he was wobbly. There was a huge rift between the families around that time. Grandpa urged me to leave, and the Reeves cut all communication. They just couldn't deal with their son's gambling.'

'Jeez, Mum, it sounds awful.'

'Yes, it was. But he was such a good person, apart from that one thing. I really miss him, you know, despite everything.'

'I know. Me too.'

'Are you furious with me?'

'Nah, not any more. I can see why telling me would have been difficult but I'm glad I know. It makes him more real.'

We turned a necessary corner that night, my mother and I, and we began to live more truthfully together.

onwards

I know I'm starting to get well again when I start daydreaming about food. I'm over smoothies. I want things I can chew. I start with simple food like wholegrain toast with honey, and crunchy salads. It's good to have an appetite again.

Who I'd like to invite to dinner

Frida Kahlo • Amelia Earhart • Emily Pankhurst
Georgia O'Keeffe • The Buddha • Janis Joplin
Ho Chi Minh • Hunter • Mel • Mum • My father

My dinner party menu

Champagne. Water from a clear mountain stream
Stuffed eggs. Asparagus rolls
Salmon with buttery mashed potatoes
Tofu for Mel
Salad with olives, fetta and avocado
Fresh raspberries and cream
Chocolates shaped like clouds

I'm on the mend. I'm nearly better. Time to get back into my life.

The day I return to school Mel's away with a cold. I'm glad. It's easier to be by myself than to fake a friendliness I don't feel for her right now. At lunch time I overhear Poppy, Caris and Emma talking about camp.

'Wasn't it hilarious, the bark thing?'

'Totally.'

'What about the pig's head?'

Mel's told me about the bark thing. They rubbed beef jerky on a piece of bark, and tied scraps of jerky on it with thread, so Carly would think it was beef jerky and eat it. Luckily for her, Mr Colgan sprung them. As for the pig's head, Finn found it under a tree. No one knew whether it had fallen off a butcher's truck or was part of some bizarre satanic ritual, but it became the highlight of the camp. The guys played soccer with it, decorated it, scared people with it and finally sent it out to sea on a makeshift raft.

I almost go over and join in, but they've moved on to discussing fake tanning products. I hesitate, and the moment's gone. Mel and I have always judged those three as shallow and boring. Today I see a group of friends sitting in the sunshine talking, and I wonder what it would be like to be

things you either

part of their crew. Easy to trash them. Not so easy to face my awkwardness. I slouch back to class by myself.

The best thing that happened that day was that Mr Colgan liked my Almodóvar essay. *Intelligent and insightful. 87%.* Clever me. When 3 o'clock came I didn't feel like going home, so I went to visit Grandad. He made a fresh brew and brought out the shortbread.

'Rough day?'

'Yep.'

'Want to talk about it?'

'Everything's crap at the moment. A boy I liked asked Mel out.'

'Poop,' says Grandad, which makes me giggle.

'Poop indeed.'

'Want more food? I could make you a sandwich.'

'Nah, I'm right.' I dip my shortbread into my tea and try not to think about Mel and Hunter, but Grandad's on to it.

'So, Georgia Reeves, about this bloke you liked. What's to be done?'

'Nothing. He asked Mel out so it's her he fancies, not me. End of story.'

'How foolish of him. Shall we hire a hitman? I could dispose of the body in the garden. Great compost.'

'Nah, better not. I'll get over it, I guess. Life sucks sometimes, though, doesn't it?'

'Indeed, sometimes it does.'

❦

On Thursday, Mel went to see *Lost in Translation* with Hunter.

'What was it like?' I ask, when I see her.

'Not bad. Some good bits but it never quite went anywhere.'

'So much for the movie. How did it go with Hunter?' I try to sound as though it's just an idle query.

'Not bad. Some good bits but it never quite went anywhere.'

'Meaning?'

'Meaning, Hunter's interesting but I'm not sure I want to have a relationship with him. Time will tell. By the way, he's having some crew over Saturday night. You're invited.'

'Nah, I don't want to go. I'm not going to any more parties.'

'It's not a party. It's just a few people and some videos. Hunter especially said to ask you. You can meet some of the Metro crowd. Please, just for me?'

'God, Mel. What's it to you?'

'It'll be fun. I want you to.'

'Oh all right,' I say grudgingly. 'Against my better judgement, I'll come.'

'Mum said she'll drive us. Pick you up around eight, okay.'

I don't want to go to the video night. I don't want to go anywhere, except perhaps Italy. I want to go to bed, with hot chocolate and my Matisse book. But if I don't go, I'll be admitting failure. I have come to a fork in the road, and I have to take it. I can't stay home feeling sorry for myself forever.

I hunt around in my wardrobe for something to wear. I try on everything I've got, in every possible combination. It all looks crap. My podgy girl clothes are too big. The stuff that does fit looks rank on me. I'm lying on my bed

things you either

surrounded by a mountain of discarded clothes when Mum comes in.

'What's up, you?'

'I've got nothing to wear to this stupid video night at Hunter's place. I don't even want to go. I've been pretending I don't mind that he and Mel are an item and Mel believes me. What am I going to do? I don't want to look dreadful.'

'I know what you need, Georgia Reeves. You need retail therapy. Come on, let's go shopping.'

❤

Shopping can be the pits, but today it's pure joy. We go to Florentino, and there it is. My dream dress. Black crepe with white flowers, skirt cut on the bias. I have to admit, I look good in it. The girl wraps it in tissue paper and tucks it in a posh carry bag.

'This one's on me,' says Mum. 'Every girl needs a wonderful dress. Come on, let's get some afternoon tea while my credit card's still quivering.'

The Savoy is an old-fashioned tea room with dark wood panelling and a floral carpet. The waitresses look like aunties, and wear pale green uniforms. There are large arrangements of lilies and gladioli, and scrummy cakes under glass domes. We order vanilla tea for two and a huge piece of carrot and walnut cake with cream-cheese icing. It arrives with two tiny silver forks and a lavish swirl of cream. We talk about Mum's work. The accountant's wife has just had triplets, two of whom have colic.

'Bags not babysitting,' I grin.

'Oh, you piker. Well, I do love afternoon tea,' says Mum. 'It should be compulsory.'

'Yes, afternoon tea is a fine thing,' I agree, scooping up the remains of the cream and the last crumbly morsel of cake. 'As fine a thing as a shooting star or a Natural Affinity tune.' We hang out for ages, reading glossies, until Mum says she's got the weekly grocery shop to do.

'Meet me at the car in half an hour?' she says.

'Good plan.'

⚘

The only store that interests me is Magazino, which sells magazines and funky stationery. My yellow journal is nearly finished so I buy a new one. Big pages, without lines. Dark green cover. Black ribbon for a bookmark. It's $29.95, but what the hell. Now that I don't need the money for the concert I might as well spend some of it.

'Hey, Georgia.'

It's Hunter. Standing right in front of me, in a blue shirt and baggy shorts, carrying a brown takeaway bag.

'Pesto scroll?' I ask. World's dumbest opening line.

'Cheddar twist. Bakery here doesn't do scrolls. These aren't bad, though.'

'So, how's life?' I ask. Second dumbest thing. My mouth is working but my brain is in a coma.

'Okay. Coming over tonight?'

'Yeah.'

We stare at each another in silence. Suddenly my mouth takes off without me again.

'That guy you saw me with, it wasn't the way it looked. I *was* going with Mel to Chocolate Fish to check out the food. It's just that the café belongs to Adrian's parents so he picked me up. He's not my boyfriend or anything. Far from it.'

156   *things you either*

'Why are you telling me this?'

'F*cked if I know,' I say. Then I turn and walk away. I make it as far as the car before I burst into tears. When Mum arrives she's in a tizz because she's misplaced her credit card and I've more or less pulled myself together, so she doesn't notice my red eyes. Blurting that out to Hunter is pretty much the most mortifying thing that's ever happened to me, and I'm not about to go public with it. No way.

♥

As soon as I get home I ring Mel to say I'm not going, but I don't tell her what happened in the car park. Every time I think about it my heart sinks and my brain hurts.

'I can't make it tonight, Mello.'

'I *knew* you were going to try and wriggle out of it, Georgia. Don't even think about it! You're coming, that's all there is to it.'

I don't want to tell her my reason, and I can't think of a convincing lie. I keep saying I'm not going but Mel keeps hassling until I give in.

'Okay, if you insist.' I hang up. It's going to be shite, but what else is new?

'You look fabulous, sweetie,' Mum says when I come down just before eight, wearing my dress. I've twisted my hair up in a tortoiseshell clasp, with a few curls hanging down.

'Thanks. Going anywhere tonight, Mum?'

'Not sure. Penny's off to Folk Club. I might tag along.'

'You should go. You need to get out more, meet people.'

'Yes, you're right,' she replies, but vaguely, because she's looking for a recipe for the quinces Joy has given her. 'I'm feeling domestic. I might bake these with honey, take some to Dad.'

'You'll never meet the man of your dreams if you don't socialise, Mama.'

'Thanks for the good advice, wise one.'

'No extra charge.' I head upstairs, admire myself in the mirror one last time, squirt on some perfume. Courage, fragrant flower.

❦

Right on eight Mel's mother arrives and off we go. Mel is wearing baggy hemp trousers and her vegan t-shirt: a cartoon of three cows holding signs saying 'Eat More Chicken'. When we pull up outside Hunter's house I panic, but Mel's mother is driving away so there's no escape. We go down the side of the house into a shed, which is Hunter's room. There are quite a few people milling around. I don't know any of the Metro crowd, but I spy Leah, Logan, Hunter and, surprisingly, Eva. Even more surprisingly, Logan has his arm draped around her. I can't keep up with her butterfly love-life but at least she's got one.

'Hiya,' says Hunter. 'Have some punch. We're about to watch *Mars Attack.*' He doesn't look at me directly when he hands me my drink, thank goodness.

'Is this alcoholic?' Mel asks.

'Yeah, but not very,' Hunter replies.

'Got any plain orange juice?' she asks, handing back the punch.

'Sure, I'll get you some.'

I'm gazing round, looking anywhere but at Hunter, so I notice Logan's face when Mel asks for orange juice. He

things you either

rolls his eyeballs. Logan's never liked Mel. Their values are directly opposite. Capitalism versus Greenpower.

'Movie time,' Leah yells, and we make ourselves comfortable on the saggy sofa, the double bed and the big pile of cushions on the floor. I sit beside Mel on the sofa; Hunter sits on the other side of her. They don't hold hands, for which I am glad. Chips and dips are passed around, and so is a joint. Not everyone takes a toke, and I hand it straight to Leah. It's going to be hard enough getting through tonight without being wasted.

The smoke must make the movie more bearable; the stoners really get off on the exploding dogs. I find it quite silly and am glad when it's over, and the music is pumped up. Some people peel off to another party and a feral girl from Metro arrives, wearing a tunic and trousers of hot orange sari fabric, which match her colorful dreadlocks. She is carrying two large pizza boxes.

'Hey, Sunflower. What you got?'

'Satay Chicken and Meat Lover Supreme, courtesy of Gerald.'

'Who's Gerald?' I whisper to Mel.

'Her brother, I think,' she whispers back.

'Yo Gerald,' grins Hunter.

'He might come by later, after work. Where shall I put these?'

❤

The pizza is delicious. Everyone hoes in, except Mel. It must be hard being vegan. Since the fish incident Mel has been more vigilant than ever. Her willpower is very strong. Even though greasy junk food is bad for you, it tastes and smells terrific. I take the largest slice of pizza and bite into it with relish. Hang in, Georgia. Soon you can go home, I remind myself.

Hunter sticks in another video, a Bollywood movie. No one actually sits down to watch but it's good eye candy. The tunes are pumping out. Leah and Sunflower get up and dance. Mel and Hunter disappear outside. I try not to think about them snogging. Logan and Eva are passing a small bottle of whisky back and forwards, slugging it down. I'm looking for ways to make the time pass quicker, so I pick the glasses up off the floor, chuck the pizza boxes in the rubbish bin, then snuggle down on the sofa to read *Mad* magazines. It seems like hours before Mel and Hunter return, but it's probably only twenty minutes. They're standing in the doorway surveying the scene when a storm starts to brew.

'So, Mel, I see you're into saving the one-legged whales. That's very noble of you,' Logan says aggressively. His voice is too loud and his face is flushed. The room goes quiet. Everyone's waiting to see how Mel will handle him.

'Pardon?' She's taken by surprise. Logan lurches towards her, jabbing the air.

'Peace, love and save the chickens.'

'Calm down, Logan,' says Eva, grabbing his arm, but he shrugs her off.

'There's no harm in Mel and me having a discussion, is there? The world's in a mess, living on carrots won't help. Big ups to a nice juicy steak, I say. All this animal liberation stuff is bollocks if you ask me.'

'I didn't ask you,' Mel says.

'Yeah, cool it, man,' Hunter adds, but Logan's drunk and he's looking for trouble.

'Can't speak for herself, then? Has to get her t-shirt and her boyfriend to do the talking?'

things you either

If he hadn't said that, Mel would probably have ignored him. But he did. And she didn't.

'Listen up, Logan. This planet is polluted because of idiots like you who don't respect the environment. As for eating dead flesh, go right ahead. Ignore the cruelty and suffering you cause innocent animals. Entire rainforests are being destroyed so beef cattle can graze. Can't you see the connections? Join up the dots, dickhead. Your choices on this planet affect everyone, whether you like it or not. What would you like written on *your* t-shirt. Too thick to care?' Mel moves towards him, her face pale with fury.

'Bravo. At least she walks her talk.' Sunflower is the first to speak. 'I admire her for that.'

'You're just a mad cow,' blusters Logan.

'Come on,' says Eva. 'Let's get some fresh air.'

'Whatever.' He nearly falls into a bean bag as he stumbles out the door.

'Yes, well,' says Hunter. 'That was pretty heavy. Um, does anyone want some coffee?'

'I do,' I say.

'Me too. I'll help you,' Leah joins in. The party vibe has definitely been eroded. Several people get ready to leave. 'Thanks, man.'

'Yeah, see ya.'

✿

Now there's only a few of us left: me, Leah, Hunter, Sunflower, Mel, and a sleepy guy called Dave. Sunflower and Mel sit cross-legged on the cushions. They're instant soul mates, deep in conversation about genetic modification. I take my coffee outside and settle back on a plastic sun lounge. There's no sign of Logan and Eva. It's peaceful here in the quiet night. I could rename the stars. I could... I could talk to Hunter because here he is, plonking himself down on the lawn beside me.

'Hey,' I say, for lack of anything better.

'I more or less stuffed that up,' Hunter says. I've no idea what he's referring to but I'm glad he hasn't mentioned the car park incident. Anything he wants to talk about is fine by me.

'Stuffed what up?'

'The interaction inside. Mel's pissed off with me, says I'm in avoidance mode. Apparently me saying "heavy" was not to her liking.'

'Don't mind Mel. She takes saving the planet very seriously. Her convictions can be daunting.'

'The thing is, she's right. I do avoid conflict.'

'How come?'

'That's the way we play it in my family. My stepfather's an expert at not dealing with things. He's laid-back to the point of apathy. It drives my mother nuts.'

'I don't have a father. He died when I was little. I live with my mother.'

'My real dad's alive and well but because he lives in Brissie I don't see him very often. We email, though.'

'Do you like your stepfather?'

'He's okay. I'm used to him now. My mother met him not long after she and my dad split up. He and I rub along, most of the time.'

'Families are weird, right?'

'Yeah, totally.'

'I might write a list about it. I'm into lists.'

'Lists? Give me an example.'

things you either

'Well, okay. It could be a list of your favourite people, or the things you want to do when you grow up.'

'I get it. How about a list of possible list topics, such as *What dogs would like to tell humans?*' Hunter suggests. Cool. He's a list-maker.

'You got it. *Great ways to cheat at Scrabble.*'

'*Scary sexual habits of insects.*'

'*Fifty ways to cook pumpkin.*'

'Um…*Worst songs to play at weddings.*'

'I like it. How about *Bad names for cats!*'

♥

I could have sat there all night talking to Hunter but Mel interrupted.

'There you are,' she says, as if nothing has happened. 'Sunflower's great,' she continues. 'We've got heaps in common.'

I feel a sharp stab of jealousy. I wish I could be the perfect world citizen, like Mel, but I can't. I'm just me, flawed and uncertain of my ideas. Rationally I agree with Mel, but I find it hard to refuse a bacon sandwich. There's a sudden burst of tooting from the street.

'It's Mum, right on time.' Mel grabs her bag.

'See ya, Hunter,' we say in unison.

'See ya,' he waves.

♥

When I get home, Mum is tucked up on the couch in her kimono, reading.

'Hi Mum. Did you go to Folk Club?'

'Nah, I delivered the stewed quinces. Dad and I talked about Michael. He told me some things I didn't know. Or

hate or love   163

maybe I did know but didn't want to acknowledge. Anyway, it clarified some things for me. He reckons you and I have misplaced our affections. You on Jakob, me on my flawed memories.'

'What did you say?'

'I admitted he might have a point.'

'Very good,' I say. 'You can borrow my new dress when you start dating, as long as you don't lose it.' I grin at her. 'Hey Mum, I had the best time tonight. And guess what – Mel and Hunter are no longer an item.'

'You guys are worse than Coronation Street,' Mum says.

I wander off to bed before she can ask me anything else. No more questions, Mama. I don't have any answers.

the graveyard shift

On Sunday afternoon Mrs Jakovich called to say she had an emergency on her hands. Could I possibly come in and do the graveyard shift, six till eleven? The twins have let her down again. She offers to pay me the overtime rate. I'm tired, but what the hell. I could use the money, I guess.

No wonder they call it the graveyard shift. The place is almost deserted. Only the odd choose to shop at this time. Mrs J has gone home and Otto's in charge. Hunter's there too.

'Hello, twin replacement,' he greets me in that soft slow way of his.

'I enjoyed the video night. What time did you sleep till?'

'Oh, I got up early. Early afternoon.'

'Lucky for some,' I reply, yawning. Otto puts Hunter, me and Leah on Check-outs 8, 9 and 10, and closes the others. I entertain myself by observing customers, like the cool couple.

things you either

She has elegant frosted hair, he wears Mambo and a silver necklace. They buy sun-dried tomato paste and artichoke hearts. She snarls. He glares. I guess you can't buy happy.

A designer dyke comes through my aisle. Butch haircut. Cool leather jacket. She buys three types of chocolate, super tampons, a *House and Garden*. This girl knows how to pamper herself when she's hormonal.

I say hi to Tom Wilson, who lives near us and goes to Amnesty meetings with Mum. Mel would love his t-shirt. *Pigs can Fly, The Earth is flat and Nuclear Power is safe.* He buys sad man groceries: a frozen curry, two mandarins, a tin of cat food.

By half past nine there aren't enough customers to keep three lines going, so Otto closes all the check-outs except Leah's. He tells Hunter to unpack cartons and asks me to take down the Specials notices, then he goes out the back to sit on a box and smoke cigarettes.

I'm so tired. My feet hurt. My brain hurts. I check out the time. Only quarter to ten. How am I going to survive another hour and a quarter?

I'm taking down the last few notices in the chilled foods area when I notice a man getting himself a drink. Late twenties, goatee beard, jeans, t-shirt, black beanie. He picks up a Red Bull, puts it down. Coca-Cola and chocolate milk, ditto. Finally he chooses juice and heads for the check-out. I follow him so that when he's gone I can chat to Leah. I stand at the top of Aisle 10, trying not to seem as if I'm lurking, even though I am. The dude hands over

hate or love   165

his juice. Leah scans it, asks him for $1.80. He gives her a two dollar coin. As she opens the till to get his change he lunges at her. Oh shit, it's a hold-up.

I watch in dismay as the guy shoves Leah roughly against the wall. She calls out something, but it's muddled. Not words. An animal noise, a guttural sound of pure fear. The man grabs the till, clumsily. Coins rattle to the floor but the notes are held in by metal clips. Leah tries to scramble up but he pushes her back, harder this time. *Stay down, he'll hurt you* – the words are loud in my mind but my lips won't move. The desperado yanks out the till, tucks it under his arm and sprints towards the door.

When he's gone I'm so shocked that I can't move. I watch, frozen, as Leah picks herself up. Everything is in slow motion, like a dreadful ballet. I see Leah rise; her fingers pulling her blue cardigan across her body in a useless protective gesture. Everything is very quiet and still, until suddenly my brain and body kick in with a huge adrenaline rush.

'Page Otto,' I yell. 'Leah. Page Otto. Now!'

Suddenly Hunter is right beside me.

'Come on!' He grabs my arm and we make chase. I can't seem to run properly, my body just won't perform. Hunter races ahead, pounding like a maniac, but the guy's really booting it. He's already halfway across the deserted car park, there's no chance of catching up. As he jumps into a white Commodore the guy behind the wheel guns the motor and they zoom away.

'Jesus,' says Hunter. We just stand there, two broken puppets with no one pulling our strings. My heart pounds with fright. A police car arrives, lights flashing. Everything is still

things you either

playing in slow motion, silent and liquid, as the police usher us inside. The shop's been cleared of customers. Leah is sitting on the floor crying. The police herd everyone into the staff room and start asking questions. When I give them a description of the thief, the senior cop congratulates me, saying I have a good eye for detail, but I'm talking too fast and adding things that aren't relevant, like what drinks the guy nearly chose. I'm in shock. I put my arm round Leah to comfort her. Hunter and Otto stand quietly to one side. Otto takes out a cigarette, then shoves it back into his pocket, bending it. Tobacco shreds spill down his shirt. Everything feels odd, clumsy and wrong.

Enquiries complete, the police depart. They take Leah to hospital because her arm is hurting badly and she can't stop crying. Otto rings our parents and asks them to pick us up. He has to fill out a report so he leaves me and Hunter in the foyer to wait. We snuggle together on the bench and go over the night's events, trying to make sense of it.

'I wish we could have done something.'

'Nothing we could have done.'

'No, I suppose not. Poor Leah.'

'Nothing prepares you for this, does it?'

'Nah.'

'Thank goodness he didn't have a weapon.'

'For real.'

Words. Useless as buckets with holes in.

Mum fusses. She makes me hot milk with honey and tucks me in like she used to when I was little.

'Want me to sing to you? You used to like me singing to you.'

'Nah,' I say. 'Raincheck on the singing. I'll be okay. Truly. Night Mum.'

I lie awake in the dark tucked under my soft covers. I can hear a song but it isn't my mother singing. *Daddy's going to buy you a diamond ring.* I was four years old. It was summer. Once upon a time when everything was safe.

♥

I dream about the robbery. It's a very clear dream.

He lingers by the freezer, but I've got his number. Not only is he acting suspiciously but the word THIEF is written on his forehead in big purple letters. I charge at him and snatch his beanie, pushing him to the ground, holding him there with my black Doc Martin boot and pouring milk over him until he begs for mercy. He whimpers pathetically and tries to grab his soggy beanie. The police arrive and tie him up, only they aren't actual people, they're dachshunds wearing uniforms. They hustle him away. I'm left alone, mopping up the milk, surrounded by thousands of cans of rice pudding.

All of a sudden I'm awake, marooned between midnight and morning. My bed is a mess. The sheet is crumpled and damp. I've been hugging one pillow; the other has tumbled to the floor. I get up to pee, then rearrange my bedding and hop in, but now I'm wide awake. I can't get comfortable – toss and turn, adrift in shadowy waters. Feverish and heavy, bruised by the intensity of the robbery and my crazy dream.

♥

When I wake, I feel surprisingly buoyant. Mum's already up, reading the paper. I make toast and coffee. I'm glad to be alive and well, and I'm not taking anything for granted this morning.

'I don't want to work at New World any more,' I say. Mum looks up, concerned.

'I'm going to ring Mrs Jakovich and tell her I quit.'

'I totally understand.'

'It's not about the robbery. I just don't like working there. It's tiring and boring. I wouldn't mind a job, but not that one.'

'Well, it's up to you, love,' says Mum. She looks a bit puzzled but she goes with it, and returns to reading the paper.

The phone rings. It's Hunter.

'How are you doing?'

'Not bad actually. I'm not going to let this totally freak me out. How are you?'

'I'm cool. Going to school today?'

'I guess so. Why?'

'I was thinking of taking the day off. Want to come along?'

'I'd like that.' I take a deep breath. It's now or never. 'Hunter, there's something I wanted to tell you last night, before the robbery bent everything out of shape.'

'What?'

'The reason I told you about Adrian was that I fancy you. Like mad.'

'What a coincidence.' I can taste his smile. 'I feel the same about you.'

♥

So we go to the park, the three of us. Me, Hunter and his basketball. I love watching him shoot baskets. He tries so hard to impress me, and blushes when he misses. Then we go to Video World, get the latest *Lord of the Rings* video and go back to my place. I make avocado and vegemite sandwiches and we set off for Middle Earth. The battles go on too long for my taste, but I like the hobbits, and the scenery is amazing. It's extremely nice sitting on the couch together, holding hands. When the credits finish rolling, Hunter nuzzles into my neck but I wriggle away. If I get a love bite I won't be able to avoid Mum's contraception lecture, which I can pretty much do without.

Instead, we kiss. It's a scrumptious kiss. It tastes good and it feels right and I want another one.

We have the best afternoon. We talk about our lives and our loves and our hates. I show Hunter my journal; he shows me his tatty old notebook of poems. I even get up the courage to ask him something.

'How come you go from girl to girl? First you were hanging around Kate, then came Eva, then you asked Mel out. Now me. What's that all about?'

'I wasn't hanging around Kate. I just came to the bakery for the pesto scrolls. Eva, well, hooking up with her was not a good idea but when she showed interest it was…tempting, I guess. Once the initial buzz wore off, I tried to get out of it as gently as I could. As for Mel, we just both wanted to see the same movie. Nothing doing there, I assure you. You're the one for me.'

'Really? Don't bullshit me, Hunter.'

'I'm not. I was keen on you right from the start. It took me ages to find out your name. I thought of you as the feisty girl with mad hair and a kick-arse attitude. When I saw you with Adrian that day I backed off because it seemed the attraction was one-sided.'

'Yeah, well, you were wrong.' I grin. 'About us, though. I

don't want to be picked up and put down like an unwanted gift.'

'Let's make a deal. We hang together for as long as it feels good. We don't lie to each other and we treat each other with respect.'

'Deal.'

'I'm getting a dog,' Hunter tells me. 'In a fortnight, when he's old enough to leave the kennel. His name's Jethro.'

'Lovely,' I say, my finger tracing the thin green line of his tattoo. 'So is this. How come you chose this design?'

'It's a Celtic cross. Some say it means eternity, or that it represents God's love. Others say it's an ancient Druid symbol. But I just chose it because I like it.'

It turns out we both have Irish ancestry. Hunter's got German and French as well. I only know that my nana came from County Cork. I think Grandpa's family came from Britain, and have no idea about my other grand-parents. I'd like to find out more. Perhaps there were interesting people in my family, way back when.

I ask Hunter about his mother. Her name is Tricia, she's thirty-seven, works in a health food shop, plays netball, loves to sew. His sister, Simone, is eleven and plays the guitar. Hunter likes history, music, dogs, surfing, skating, camping, science fiction, soccer, basketball, and me.

We're sitting happily hand-in-hand on the couch when Mum arrives home, very excited because she has a present for me. I open it carefully, smoothing the silvery wrapping paper down so it can be used again. It's a camera. A Pentax.

'You have a good eye,' says my mother. 'I think you'll make a fine photographer.'

'Man, that is very cool,' says Hunter, and helps me figure out how to put the film in.

'Over here please,' I command, feeling rather professional.

Mum and Hunter standing against a plain white wall. Mum in her straw gardening hat and Hunter in his skate cap. My very first photo.

this new life

I love photography. I join a night class that Poppy goes to. She's got a digital camera, and likes experimenting with odd effects: double exposures and weird fuzzy landscapes with kaleidoscopic edges. The teacher, Tim, is from Manchester. He has a loud laugh which matches his loud shirts. He brings along wonderful books and encourages us to look at things in new ways. Creativity gets hold of me. It has its own energy. I'm interested in colour, shape and light, in shadows and edges. I write lists and poems in my new journal, but it's also a visual diary, a place for my photographs and their titles. I add texture: a blue-green feather, a fragment of old lace. I draw borders with soft smudgy pencils: colourful repeating patterns that would make great textiles, or wallpaper. I don't want to limit myself to one art form. Photographer, writer, designer, I plan to be all of them and more.

Things I Photograph
    Mel and Sunflower, holding a Peace banner
        (*girls save world*)
    Rows of shopping trolleys (*metal sculpt buy*)
    Hunter skateboarding (*boy air dancing*)
    Mrs Jellicoe and her handbag made of zips
        (*have purse, will travel*)

Things I Can't Photograph
the pot of gold at the end of the rainbow
the inside of a walnut
janis joplin eating breakfast
the quack of a duck
how chocolate tastes
the smell of a dirty sock
ghosts and angels
my own bottom
hunger
how I feel about my father
music
the softness of a petal
a rat the size of the empire state building dressed
    up as santa claus

rodent city

I love my new job. I wanted it the minute I saw it in the paper, so I wrote a proper CV for it. Decided it was best not to send my earlier one. The interview was a breeze. They asked some very basic questions, then said 'When can you start?'

Every Sunday afternoon I wander across the campus, pretending to be a uni student. When I come to the door marked Bio-Medical Research Lab, I press the seven-digit code, open the door and there they are. My babies: 347 rats. A medical student named Olga looks after the 5002 mice and a sheep called William. She works mornings, so it's just me and my rats. I blast up the radio, put on my rubber shoes and medical scrubs, then get to work. I clean the cages, keeping my babies safe in a big carton, five at a

time, while I change the straw. When I've finished cleaning I top up the grain pellets. Then I hang out with Jakob,
my pet of pets. He has a genetic variation that means he's
larger than your average rat and sports a tiny fur Mohawk
tuft. His deluxe cage, the Rat Ritz, is stocked with toys I've
constructed from cardboard tubes and egg cartons. Jakob
enjoys mirrored surfaces, stairs, tunnels and anything that
rolls. Sometimes I put another rat in with him but he's an
introvert. He doesn't really like to mingle.

❤

Mel and I are drifting apart. We tried to talk about what
happened at the party but it felt awkward.

'You and Hunter didn't stand up for me. You wouldn't
speak out. The world needs improvement. If people won't
take a stand then nothing changes.'

'I'm not the enemy, Mel. Everyone has to do what feels
right to them. You can't force someone to feel the same as
you.'

'I'm not trying to force you, or anyone else. I'm trying to
encourage you. Want to come to the rally with me and
Sunflower on Sunday?'

'Can't. I'm working.'

Mel sniffed. She doesn't approve of my new job. I've
explained to her that the animals are well treated, that the
research leads to knowledge and medical advances, but she
still thinks animal research is wrong.

It's hard to let go of a friendship, or at least to let it
change shape. I miss the way things used to be. I tried to
talk to Mel about it again when I felt calmer, but she didn't
respond, just began describing the vegan cookbook she and
Sunflower plan to write. Sometimes I think Mel's more

things you either

interested in ideas than in people, but I miss her anyway. She was my first best friend. We shared a lot.

These days I spend my lunchtimes in the art department. I read the photography books, or use the darkroom. Poppy and I hang out together, when she's around.

❤

Joy and Kevin were both gutted about the split but they lived apart for a few months while they sorted things out. Uncle Kev got himself a better haircut and several nice shirts. He even went to Table for Six, where he met a physiotherapist named Ruth, who had curly red hair and two cats. When Aunty Joy heard about Ruth she decided she'd had enough space. She asked Uncle Kevin to come home and try again. Reeled him back in again, as Penny so elegantly put it. Gilda has applied to Volunteer Service Abroad. She wants to work in Africa, helping villagers build solar ovens. What about teaching computer skills in Fiji? I asked her. Not far enough away, she replied, and who can blame her.

❤

Mum went out with Tom Wilson, the guy who goes to her Amnesty Meetings. Only once though. They went to dinner and a movie.

'How did it go?' I asked when she came home. I was watching *Ever After* on TV but it was the ad break so I had a minute to spare.

'Okay.'

'Just okay?'

'Yeah.'

She and Penny are starting Tango classes, so maybe she'll meet someone there.

Sooze is seeing a guy named Gerald who breeds goats. She emailed Mum asking if she could bring him to visit us. Three days max, Mum reckons, and don't bring the goats.

Finn still loves Hannah. He's turning into a sad case. I saw him one night, drunk, writing his name on a shop window with a hot chip.

Hannah is seeing Max, an exchange student from Canada.

Caris loves Dan.

Logan loves Natalie.

Emma is wondering if she is bi.

Poppy has the hots for the DJ at Midnight.

Toby is still in love with Mel.

Mel loves the earth, the sky and the dolphins.

Soon I'll be sixteen. I've had my hair cut, short and feathery. It suits me, Hunter says. I wear mainly black these days. I scored the best velvet coat, black with maroon silk lining, at a garage sale. You have to have the right look if you're going to be a famous film-maker. Hunter brought Jethro home. That dog is pure joy.

At Christmas, Hunter and I are going to Brisbane. He's going to visit his dad and I'm going to stay with the Reeves. Maybe they won't be as revolting as I remember. No harm in giving them another chance. I'm older now. I see things differently. I'm keen to talk to them about my father and our family history, before it's too late.

things you either

Being with Hunter isn't perfect, but it's pretty fine. I've abandoned my blue moon dancer fantasy and I've settled for a true friend who makes me laugh. The fact that his kisses taste better than chocolate doesn't hurt either. We're hoping for a few nights at the Brisbane Youth Hostel, just the two of us, but we're still working on that part.

❖

One full moon night Hunter and I make a ritual. Under the leafy canopies of trees in the Botanical Gardens we light sparklers and write our names in the sky. Then we circle the magnolia tree three times, dig a hole, say a few words.

'Here's to the future.'

'Here's to the past, and the present.'

'Here's to hidden things.'

'Here's to us.'

Jethro gives a small bark.

I place my old journal in a tartan biscuit tin, along with my dried seahorse, the ruby earring, and a photograph of us taken the day I had my hair cut. Hunter adds a plastic figurine of a skateboarder and his toilet paper poem. I write 'With Lots of Love from Georgia' on the back of an Edward Weston postcard. Hunter scratches *Mad hair girl & Air wind boy = Happy* on a leaf. We seal the tin with candle wax and bury it deep. One day someone will find it, somewhere in the future, that mysterious place where anything can happen.

Ways I could spend my $$$ now that Natural Affinity have hit the dust

Buy a golden bicycle

Fold it into tiny paper cranes like Sadako

Roll it up to snort cocaine (only kidding Mum)

Light a bonfire and burn it in a pagan rite

Give it to Amnesty

Give half to Amnesty and blow the rest on a carved Balinese day bed

Buy ninety-seven Lotto tickets

Buy cherries for my father. Mum and I could sit by his grave and eat cherries and talk to him. That would be good.

things you either

things to do while watching a sunset

    sing a Ben Harper song
    clean nails with a twig
    name the clouds
    yawn
    sneeze
    wriggle toes
    compose a small poem
    play marbles
    write your name in air with your finger
    pray for world peace
    practise winking
    make a daisy chain
    eat a peach
    share a picnic
    drink something fizzy & burp a lot
    kiss or be kissed
    laugh out loud because in 300 years
        your zits will not matter

BRIGID LOWRY is a poet and novelist. Her wry and true-to-life writing has garnered her previous novels, *Guitar Highway Rose* and *Follow the Blue*, much praise. *Guitar Highway Rose* was a New York Public Library Book for the Teen Age and *Kirkus Reviews* lauded it as "sure to be an instant hit with teens." *Follow the Blue* was called "exhilarating," by *Booklist* in a starred review, which went on to say, "A lot goes on in this very funny romp, some of it quite profound, and Lowry manages to remain mercifully nonpreachy throughout." A native of New Zealand, she also teaches creative writing and enjoys traveling, nectarines, sleeping in, and colored pencils.